PLAYING WITH PHYRE

GRAHAM MARKS

Catnip

To Andrea, for the green light,
and Non for making it all come together.

CATNIP BOOKS
Published by Catnip Publishing Ltd.
14 Greville Street
London EC1N 8SB

This edition first published 2010
1 3 5 7 9 10 8 6 4 2

This edition (based on an original storyline published as *Haden's Quest*, copyright © 1996 Graham Marks) © 2010 Graham Marks
The moral right of the author has been asserted.

Cover design by Mandy Norman
Cover illustration by Eamon O'Donoghue

A CIP catalogue record for this book is available from the British Library.

ISBN 978-1-84647-111-7

Printed in Poland

www.catnippublishing.co.uk

CONTENTS

Lighting the Match . . .

THE OLD MAN SAT by the window, waiting. The boy would be here soon and he was looking forward to spending some time with him. His grandson was the only person these days who enjoyed hearing his stories and he wondered, as he waited, how much longer that would remain true. He was growing up fast, the boy, and soon would have other, far better things to do than sit and listen to his grandfather's tales; even though they were of the most cutthroat and savage adventures.

Sometimes he thought maybe he should write the stories down because once he stopped telling them, they would disappear quicker than morning mist and be lost for ever. But who else would be interested? Everything had changed so much since he was a boy and the world was a different place now. It was a safer place, in many ways, but a place that never seemed to stand still; where no one had enough time. It was a world he thought of as suffering from progress like it was a disease.

There had been a world before the Union had been forged – through skirmish, battle, blood and politics – into a mighty empire, but that old world wasn't even a distant memory for most people today. They'd all but forgotten the years of brutal struggle and ferocious conflict – even his own son had only the haziest idea of what life had been like when all there had been was a wary, distrustful patchwork of Territories: the largest, Quadrine and Massenine, dominating Sektaine, Cherinna, Uskarnha and the rest. All were now parts of a larger whole, while some regions, like the Outlands, had been absorbed and had completely disappeared . . . gone, like so many of the people who had fought and died to create the Union.

Shrugging, the old man glanced across the room and caught his reflection in a mirror on the far wall; he'd been told that his white hair, long and pulled back in a thin plait, and his trimmed white beard gave him the look of a scholar and a sage. The idea, as it always did, made him smile, deep lines radiating out from the corners of his faded blue eyes.

'A scholar!' he said mockingly to his mirror image. 'Only thing *I'm* an expert on is being long in the tooth . . .'

Turning back to the window he realised how much he looked forward to spending some time, even if it was only a few hours a week, with someone young, someone who didn't always have too much to do. And then the old man saw his daughter's vehicular turn into the street and he went to the door. Today was going to be different, though. Today he'd decided he was finally going to tell the boy the truth. The time had come, and his grandson was old enough now to hear the real story about how it had all started, how everything had happened.

How he'd become the person he was today.

For the old man this story, these memories – and the people who had played such important roles in his early life – were as vibrant and strong as if they'd happened yesterday, instead of decades ago. As he opened the door he stopped for a moment, thinking what an extraordinary story it was! Unbelievable, some might say. Often, when he thought back, even he found it hard to credit that it had actually happened and that he'd had a part to play. He hoped he could truly bring everything to life and do it justice . . .

'However you chose to describe Starpoint, there was no getting away from the fact that it was a small and unimportant place. A dot on the map – if there'd been a map of the Outlands then.' The old man sat back in his leather armchair, smiling, and crossed his legs in front of him. He was going to enjoy telling this tale. 'It was, to be truthful, a place to pass through on the way to somewhere else, somewhere to forget you'd ever been,' he continued, looking at his grandson, Mykel, sitting on the sofa opposite with a tray of food on the small table next to him.

'The world then was full of villages and hamlets just like Starpoint, there not quite by mistake, but only because that was where two roads happened to cross; in Starpoint's case there were three of them, which was probably the most interesting thing about it. In this place – just a scattering of houses and farms, a handful of stores and a couple of two-bit saloons – the outside world was an echo, and time meandered so slowly it almost stood still. And if Starpoint was where you came from, Mykel, that was generally where you stayed.

'But the day Haden Akatine left, it was because there was nothing there to stay for . . .'

1 A Noise in the Silence

THE EARLY MORNING HAZE was still swirling above the ground, fingers of it clinging on in some places as the sun chased it away. The village had been devastated. Plumes of smoke were rising from burnt-out houses like the thin, departing spirits of their former inhabitants and, as the seconds ticked by and the air cleared, what had looked like discarded piles of tattered clothing became bodies. Dead bodies.

If there had been a witness to these gruesome revelations, apart from a trio of inquisitive crows, they would have been in no doubt that this no-account place had, for some inexplicable reason, been subjected to a horrific and frenzied attack. And the first question to cross the mind of this witness, had they existed, would have been: *why?* What could this dull hamlet, in the middle of nowhere, possibly have done to deserve such devastation?

As the crows, emboldened by the lack of movement, began to inspect one of the bodies, its sightless eyes staring at the dusty horizon, the hand of the corpse next to it moved. The abrupt jerk sent the birds skittering into the air, along with puffy clouds of fine, grey ash.

The 'corpse' hauled itself up, first onto its knees, then stood and stared at the destruction, shivering. For a long time the lone, ghostly figure was like a statue, only its eyes moving, darting here and there, trying to make sense of the completely inexplicable.

This was no dead man walking though, no spirit trapped between the worlds of the living and the dead. It was a thin, muscular boy, tall for his age, with long hair and piercing blue eyes, and, as he stood looking at what was left of the only place he'd ever known, a tear welled up and cleared a path down the boy's ash-dusted cheek. He blinked the next one away. This was no time for crying.

The boy began to move, his feet raising clouds of ash as he stumbled first right and then left, unsure of what he should do or where he ought to look. There might be other survivors . . . there *had* to be . . . and he wanted more than anything to find them . . . to find his father, his mother, his brother – *someone*.

He had never felt this alone and abandoned. Ever. Seconds turned into minutes and as the minutes piled up it became obvious that no matter how hard he searched, the boy wasn't going to find anyone alive in the smouldering ruins of his village.

Sinking back down onto his knees, Haden Akatine finally allowed himself to grieve . . .

Starpoint was one of the smallest, most insignificant specks in the Outlands. Or at least that's how those who passed through often described it. Haden had no idea if this was true because he'd never been anywhere else. What he did know of the outside world came from the travellers and traders, always on their way to or from somewhere more exotic and interesting. Some of the stories they told fired his imagination, while others filled him with dread. The world far beyond the edge of the sky sounded both fascinating and dangerous. Like the snakes you came across out on the plateau: beautiful, but deadly.

And then yesterday, as the sun was setting, someone had spotted the riders coming in from the west. By the looks of the dust they were throwing up there were a lot of them, which should have meant some good business. This late in the day people tended to stay rather than ride on through the night to wherever they were going.

At around the time the dull rumble of the horses' hooves could finally be heard, someone in the small crowd of watchers also spotted the dull glint of dusk-light on steel: the riders had, for some reason, unsheathed their swords and unholstered their pistols. Not a good sign. To a man the watchers turned and ran.

But their warnings came too late.

The attack had been as vicious as it was short. As random as it was destructive. As bewildering as it was brutal. These riders, as the villagers had realised far too late, were a band of marauding Sardar, a breed of men who had a heartless disregard for life – their own and everyone else's – that was legendary.

And in the end Haden only survived because, in the heat of the frantic, lethal melee, he'd been battered to the ground and left, in a crumpled heap, for dead.

He didn't cry for long. There wasn't much point. His whole world was in ruins, his entire family – his younger brother, Quinn, his parents – were gone, along with neighbours, friends. Everyone. Shedding tears wouldn't help to bring any of them back. Nothing could do that. Then the thought struck him that he hadn't searched *every*where and it spurred him into a burst of frenzied activity that achieved little except to appal him at how cruel men could be.

Standing surrounded by his broken world, Haden found there was nowhere he could look that didn't give him pain, and it was then that he decided he had to leave. If he stayed there could be no vengeance, and he needed that like he needed air to breathe. He might die trying to get it, but no one was going to stop him finding the killers and tearing their hearts out.

Revenge. Payback. Satisfaction. He would have all three.

As the idea crystallised in Haden's mind, forming a clear picture of the punishment he would mete out, he heard a noise in the unearthly silence and he whirled around. Was it a door creaking in the lazy breeze that had come to worry the embers and the piles of ash? Or was it someone moving? Was someone alive?

'Who is it?' His voice was hardly more than a whisper and Haden almost didn't recognise it as his own.

Nothing moved, no one's reply broke the hushed, keening silence.

'Is anyone there?'

Slowly the shattered door to the cellar of a store some way down the street was pushed open and a head of badly cropped, soot-covered red hair poked up. Even from where he was standing Haden could see the familiar, slightly bewildered expression on the face staring back at him.

'Decker?' he muttered under his breathe.

Decker. Haden shook his head. Of all the people who lived in Starpoint, why, of all people, had the Fates chosen to save the village idiot? He looked away, feeling bad about thinking of the six-foot-five-inch mute this way, but that was how they'd always treated him, and now here he was, the only other survivor.

And he couldn't talk to him.

It didn't make any kind of sense but then, Haden thought as he walked towards Decker, his gaze wandering over what was left of the village, not much did any more . . .

2   INTO THE RIFT

HADEN RAN, LEGS POUNDING, arms pumping, his lungs working like a blacksmith's bellows, straining to keep him supplied with oxygen. Beside him, silently keeping pace, was Decker. Even though Deck was older than him by a good few years, Haden didn't think he'd have the wit to survive on his own, so he'd had no choice but to bring him along. On the upside, while Deck wasn't the brightest candle on the table by a long chalk, he had no problem with carrying far more than his fair share of the provisions they'd scavenged for the journey.

They'd taken water, although not a lot as it was very heavy, they had a reasonable amount of food and they had weapons (even a pistol but, unfortunately, no ammunition). Enough for at least four, maybe five, days. After that if they hadn't found their prey then Haden didn't know what he'd do. It had been a gruesome job, finding what they needed, but it had to be done even though it was stealing from the dead. Hardest had been taking the dagger from his own father's cold hand. But it *had* to be done. And if there was any justice then that dagger, now sheathed on his own belt, was the weapon he'd use to kill the first marauder they found.

As he ran, his body keeping everything going like a clockwork mechanism, Haden let his mind wander at will. In his mind's eye he could see the skeletal carcass of the village being picked over by carrion birds and foraging animals, and felt bad that he and Deck hadn't buried the dead the way they deserved, until the voice of reason reminded him that that job would have taken weeks. As it was, every hour that went by made following the trail more difficult and success less likely.

As he ran one thought kept recurring: why had Starpoint been chosen – why wipe out *his* village? But he also realised he was glad to have Deck with him. It was good to have company, even if he still had no one to talk things over with; no one to help him make sense of what had happened. Because nothing made sense. Except the running. The running numbed him, took the pain and used it to get him away from a place he knew deep down he would never see again.

•

At some point (he'd lost track of time) Haden stopped. They were by now quite far out in the Plains, an immense scrub-covered sweep of land that seemed to go on for ever no matter where you looked. They were miles from anything that might pass for a road. This was the heart of nowhere and an easy place to get lost, even if you'd grown up here, but the trail they'd been following showed no signs of hesitation. The men they were after knew where they were going. As Haden stood with Decker taking a few sips of their precious water the marauders' obvious confidence gave him an odd sense of belief that *he* also knew what he was doing.

That was a hard thing to believe, considering the facts: two people, a boy and a soft-in-the-head mute, against a troop of battle-hardened men. What chances did he and Deck have? None. That was the reality, and if that was the case, should he be taking Deck with him or even be thinking of going a step more on the journey?

'Too many questions . . .' Haden shook his head as he split a strip of dried meat in half and gave a piece to Deck. His companion nodded and shrugged. 'And not enough answers, eh, Deck?'

Decker nodded again, but looked doubtful.

'Something the matter?'

Decker made an obvious *'D'you know what you're doing?'* gesture.

'Yeah . . . right . . .' Haden looked away. Another good question, the only answer to which was: not really. He pointed at the wide slew of tracks made by the horsemen. 'Only one way to go, Deck. Got to find them and kill as many as we can!'

Decker's face lit up and he bared his teeth in a grim smile. Picking up his sack, which was twice the size of Haden's, he started running.

'Hey, Deck . . . wait for me!'

Out in the flat, drab Plains there was precious little to see. High up above them the occasional bird wheeled in a rising thermal, its wings stretched to catch the lift it needed to stay aloft. Haden spotted a couple of hawks and a buzzard or two – the latter, he thought, waiting to see if one of the boys fell to the ground and became its next meal. And then, up ahead, he noticed something odd about the tracks.

Slowing down he saw that instead of the steady, straight-line progress, it had been making, the trail became confused and the ground a chaotic, churned mess. Haden stood for some time, trying to decipher what the message written so carelessly in the dirt could mean. Followed by a curious Decker, he walked round the outer edge, circling the area and examining ground.

The Sardar had been riding fast across the Plains and had come to a halt for some reason or other. After completing his circuit, Haden was none the wiser as to why. But he did know what had happened next: they'd split up and a small group of the riders had left the main group and headed north on their own. The rest had carried on their way going more or less east.

Squatting by the trail heading north Haden knew that the odds had turned in his favour, if only in the smallest way. If he ever caught up with them, fewer men meant a lot less trouble than the whole murderous band. He stood up and saw Decker standing right next to him holding up three fingers.

'What?' Haden watched as Decker indicated the easterly trail. 'You think it's three riders, Deck?'

Decker knelt down, pointing at the ground; he counted out three fingers again, and then nodded. Haden looked more closely at the tracks.

'Could be right . . .' he said, frowning; just because Decker couldn't talk didn't mean he couldn't see. 'Right, we'll follow the three riders – come on, Deck, let's go!'

A short time after leaving the spot where the riders had split up, Haden and Decker found themselves standing at the lip of a massive, rock-strewn valley, so wide they could only just make out the other side.

The Rift. It was an awesome sight, looking like the earth had been torn and ripped apart, the valley's sides steep and pitted and a heat haze making the air ripple. This was not a welcoming place and Haden stood at the edge wishing he didn't have to go there; but since that was where the tracks led he had no choice but to follow. Haden squared his shoulders.

Decker spread his arms out as wide as they would go, and whistled.

'Bigger than big.' Haden nodded and set off.

Some way down Haden stopped. It wouldn't be *that* long before dusk, and then, he knew, night would fall like a drunk in a bar. And as the moon was still only days old, then, after that all they'd have to show the way was starlight. This would make things difficult for them, but ahead lay the kind of terrain that would make it downright dangerous for horses – one false move and your mount could break a leg and be as good as dead. If the three Sardar had any sense at all they'd be looking for somewhere to stop for the night, which, as it was going to get very cold, *might* mean a fire.

Searching the landscape, Haden let his eyes wander slowly back and forth looking for something, *any*thing that might be a sign of where their quarry might be. He was ready to give up when he felt Decker tap his shoulder. He turned and saw his friend pointing into the gathering twilight.

Haden squinted and finally caught a vague glimmer, a flicker, directly north but still some miles ahead. It was, as his father would have said, as good a bet as having four aces in your hand that there was no one else but the three marauders out there. It had to be them. Why should they care about covering their tracks and keeping their whereabouts a secret? After all, who was going to be following them?

'Well done, Deck!' Haden patted him on the back and got a beaming smile back in return.

The hunt was on.

3 His Father's Gift

THE PREVIOUS NIGHT'S JOURNEY had been a pitch-black nightmare as he and Decker had tried to cut the distance between them and the riders by carrying on long after the sun had gone down. Before they'd finally collapsed he'd laid a number of large stones together in a rough arrow shape, pointing in the direction of the faint trace of light that still glinted somewhere up ahead; the next morning they'd know which way to go.

What woke him Haden didn't know. Maybe it was the first rays of the morning sun – more probably the raw, bone-chilling cold that made it feel as if his blood had frozen – but once sleep left him, Haden was aware of nothing except his aches and pains. And then the reality hit that he had spent the night out in the Rift and not at home. Because he didn't have a home any more. Surprisingly, when Decker woke up, he appeared to feel fine and made it clear he was hungry.

Washed in the fiery gold of a late evening the Rift had looked quite picturesque but now, in the steely dawn, it was a grey, soulless desert where jagged rocks and thorn-covered bushes were the sole features to look at while they ate. When they'd finished, having eaten probably too much of their precious food store, Haden stood up with a loud groan.

Decker mimed a pained expression and pointed at him, grinning.

'Glad you think it's so funny . . .' Haden looked down at the ragged figure sitting in the ground, still smeared with the soot and grime from Starpoint. There was something about this odd man-boy that he couldn't work out – something in his eyes that made Haden wonder about what he was really like behind the often blank expression. He'd grown up with Decker, but had to admit to himself that he'd paid him less attention than the village dogs. He smiled and put his hand out. 'Time to make a move, Deck.'

Decker stood up, towering over Haden, head on one side, the faintest of smiles on his lips; he gave Haden's hand a gentle squeeze then a shake. It was a strange, haunting moment. A bond had been created, sealed by the fact that both knew they'd be lost without the other.

'Together,' Haden said, looking up. 'You and me, Deck. You and me . . .'

•

There was no way of knowing exactly where the riders' campsite was, or whether they would still be there, and the last thing Haden wanted was to be spotted. As they were about to set off he remembered a saying of his father's: *caution is what keeps a brave man alive*. Right then, out in the middle of the windswept Rift, he realised what the words *really* meant and signalled to Decker that the two of them should keep as low as they could.

Making their way through a maze of thornbrush, Haden thought more about what his father had told him over the years. He wondered about the man who was – had been – the village blacksmith, about how he'd known so much about so many things. Although his father never talked about it, others in the village sometimes told stories about the days when Akatine (he was only ever called by his family name, even by their mother) had been a fighter and a gun-for-hire.

Haden had never believed those stories, but now he began to suspect that his father had been feeding him knowledge and information since he was old enough to walk: the swordplay, the dagger games, not to mention the fact that even though they didn't own a horse (although they shod everyone else's), both he and Quinn could ride better than well. None of these pieces had made a complete picture before, but now Haden realised his father had been preparing them for a time when they might need those skills.

Slinking towards the campsite, Haden knew that this was one of those times for which his father had been planning. He knew, too, that he was going to need a lot more than just his wits about him if he was going to come out of all this alive.

When they finally reached the campsite the day had turned dull and cloudy and it had stayed cold. As soon as they saw the size of the fire the men had built (they had certainly kept themselves very warm the previous night) there was no mystery about why they'd been able to see it from so far away. The numerous thorn bushes hacked to the ground was evidence of the amount of material they'd burnt and, within the rough six-foot-wide stone circle the men had made, the pile of embers was still warm to the touch.

The riders had made no attempt to hide the fact they'd been there, and a quick search of the area turned up nothing of interest, except proof that Decker had been right: there were three of them.

The route they'd taken when they'd left appeared to follow the downward slope of the Rift, leading them towards a sandy basin that would, during the rainy season have a wide river rushing through it. Far ahead Haden could see huge rocky outcrops – massive piles of black stone rearing up out of the ground, their tops looking as if they were almost level with the edges of the plains. They looked like the kind of things giants would build, if giants existed. Which Haden was sure they didn't.

While the going got a lot easier, a couple of things made Haden worry. Firstly, a stiff breeze had sprung up, which, if it got much stronger, would begin to sweep away the trail they were following. Secondly, there would soon be much less cover.

As they ran, he heard his father's voice in his head, so clear it was almost like he was there with him. *Always follow like the fox*, he was saying, *and stay downwind.* When he'd said things like that back in Starpoint, Haden and Quinn had grinned at each other and not taken much notice. Out here he could see the wisdom in it: be sly, be wily and, above all, be the hunter. Not the hunted.

Up ahead the first of the strange outcrops was getting nearer. It was over to their right and, to Haden's surprise, the tracks they were following abruptly veered off at an angle and made straight for it. Haden stopped running, Decker pulling up next to him.

'See that, Deck?' he nodded at the trail.

Decker made an exaggerated '*Why?*' face.

'Dunno . . . we'll have to go and find out.'

But before either of them could make a move there was a loud, sharp *k-raack!* that echoed off the distant rocks. A rifle shot. It couldn't be anything else. Were the marauders fighting amongst themselves (always a possibility), or did this mean there was someone else out here?

AMBUSH

THE ECHO DIED, SLOWLY. Haden and Decker, now both crouching down, looked at each other, rooted to the ground, waiting to see what happened next. The logical thing to do, having guns but no ammunition, would be find a way around the trouble. But whatever was happening, there was no doubt the people they were following were in the middle of it. So logic was going to have to be ignored . . .

K-raack! K-raack! K-raack!

Three more shots rang out in quick succession, followed by a fourth, which ricocheted off some rock with a high-pitched metallic whine. Decker made a *'What now?'* face and Haden shrugged. He had no idea what to do next, other than get closer to observe without being seen and not get involved unless he had to. Which was when another of his father's sayings came back to him: *look*, *think*, then *do*.

He looked; as far as he could see, there was no sign of anyone on this side of the tower of rock. He thought; rather than go round the looming rock, better to go up it and get a bird's-eye view of what was going on. Time for doing. Haden moved, signalling for Decker to come with him as quietly as possible.

Haden set off, sprinting towards the black rock face, his heart beating double-quick, expecting a bullet at any moment. None came and the two of them reached the base and began climbing. The steep, almost sheer, stone reached up some eighty feet and it wasn't a climb that Haden would have undertaken lightly under normal circumstances. But his hands and feet automatically searched for and found holds, and before he knew it he was well over halfway up, with Decker not far behind.

The last twenty-five feet slowed them both down. It was even steeper and they had to be mouse-quiet. By the time he reached the top, Haden's muscles were screaming at him to give them a rest but, much as he would've loved to, he knew he had to keep moving. Finally making it onto the flat summit, Haden crawled forward, inching himself into a position where he could just peer over the north-facing lip.

For a moment he couldn't work out what was happening. Unlike the side they'd just climbed up, the northern flank of the rock tower fell away more gradually in a series of jagged layers until it reached the sandy basin of the Rift. Nothing was moving. No sign of the three men they were following, no sign of anything. Then Decker nudged Haden, pointing down and over to his left where Haden caught sight of a dead horse and, a few feet from it, the body of one of the marauders, the blood stain on his chest matching his red bandana.

Haden was just about to move forward slightly to get a better look when another shot rang out, spanking off the rocks directly below them. He jerked back, away from the edge, and glanced at Decker.

'They seen us, Deck?' he whispered.

Decker shrugged in response, just as there was a volley of return fire, closer this time and sounding more like pistol shots. Haden carefully inched forward again and sneaked a look. There, some forty feet beneath him, off to his right, he saw the remaining two riders holed up behind a rock.

One of the men fired off a couple of quick, wild shots without really aiming, with the single reply coming almost instantly from out in the scrubland. So, there was only one person out there. Haden scanned the area and almost missed a wisp of smoke fly away from a dense clump of brush a hundred yards or so away. Whoever it was appeared to have the upper hand. He'd already killed one of the riders, and his horse, and had pinned down the other two. For now.

As he watched, Haden could see the trapped men, heads together, deep in conversation. If he was in their position he knew what *he'd* do: split up. One man couldn't keep two moving targets covered at the same time and, if they were lucky, he might not even hit either of them when they took the initiative. Something that looked like it could happen at any moment.

Haden moved away from the edge. Any enemy of the these men should be treated as a friend, but how was this person to know he and Decker were on his side? If they tried to help mightn't they simply end up getting shot at themselves, possibly killed? Much good *that* would do all his grand ideas of revenge for the deaths of his family and the destruction of his home. But doing nothing wouldn't achieve much either, except make him feel bad. There was really only one way to find out.

'*Deck*!' Haden motioned him over. 'We have to help, those two down there are going to . . .'

Decker made a parting motion with his hands to show he'd also worked out what was likely to happen. Haden nodded.

'You and me have to stop them, OK?'

Decker put a thumb up and signalled that he was ready to go.

To try and ensure that they looked as little like the marauders as possible, both of them had stripped to the waist and Haden had tied his hair back. Armed only with knives, they crawled away from each other to either side of the summit of the column of rock and quietly slid over the edge. As Haden started, crab-like, to make his descent, he could still see that the two Sardar hadn't made a break for it. As soon as they did, he and Decker would make their own move. They'd stuffed their trouser pockets with as many fist-sized pieces rock as they could; it was the only ammunition they had and they planned to hurl it at the men, catch them off guard and give the rifleman a chance to shoot them both. As improvised plans went it wasn't a bad one, Haden thought, as long as the sharpshooter didn't try and pick him and Decker off first.

Four or five silent yards down. So far, so good.

Seven or eight yards. Over halfway. Still all right. But he couldn't see where Decker had got to.

Nine yards. Going very, v-e-r-y slowly, Haden reckoned whoever was behind the brush must have worked out by now whose side they were on, and it looked like the two men were about to leave the safety of their hiding place.

Nine-and-a-half yards. A shard of rock, cracked by the constant temperature changes, gave way when he stepped on it and clattered noisily down the slope.

Both the Sardar swung round to see where the sound was coming from and froze. For the longest moment they gaped up at Haden and he stared down at them in a tableau of surprised bewilderment. Then Haden found himself looking down the barrels of two pistols and he knew he was going to die. With a horrible clarity he could see fingers tightening on triggers and felt himself getting ready to do the impossible and leap back up the slope.

While fear can make you attempt almost anything, anger, on the other hand, makes you careless. One of the men, maybe incensed at what he saw as a cowardly attack, stood up and held his pistol with both hands to get a better aim. Making the back of his head a perfect target.

From where Haden was crouching, everything appeared to happen at once. A stone arced into view and smashed into the head of the man still hunkered behind the rock, who keeled over and dropped his pistol, while to Haden's intense surprise, the shot that rang out didn't kill him. Instead he saw the man pointing the gun at him jerk like he'd been punched, then crumple sideways to the ground.

Haden had no idea that bullets, which made such a small hole going in, could make such a mess coming out.

In the silence all Haden could hear was a loud, insistent pounding in his ears and it took him seconds to realise it was his own heart. Then he saw a movement and, grabbing his dagger, he leapt. With a guttural scream he fell through the air and crashed into the second man, who rolled sideways onto his back. His face, like his dead companion's, was covered in spiral-patterned dark blue tattoos, and as their eyes locked, Haden was aware that this was the first time in his whole life that he had *really* hated someone.

His father's dagger, sharpened to a razor's edge, scythed down and did its job.

Haden slowly stood up, pulling the blade out and saw Decker standing a few feet away, watching him.

'I wish I could kill him a dozen more times, Deck.' Haden spat at the body on the ground. 'It's what he deserves.'

Decker nodded, then looked over towards the straggly brush where the mystery rifleman was and made a '*Where is he?*' face.

'Good point, Deck –' Haden leaned down and cleaned his knife blade on the red bandana of the man he'd just killed, '– you go back up and fetch our gear, I'll get their guns and go and have a look.'

This was the second time in two days that Haden had stripped dead bodies of anything of value, but this time it was different, like dealing with a slaughtered animal, and he felt nothing. By the time Decker had come back down Haden had their holsters, belts, ammunition, guns, even their battered gold earrings. Together they trotted the rest of the way down the slope but as they crossed towards the thick brush, still no one appeared and Haden tensed up.

Stopping as they neared the man's cover Haden cocked the pistol he was holding.

'Hello?' he called out, listening for a reply. 'Are you all right?'

A sound . . . a groan? Someone in pain?

Without thinking it might be a trap, the two of them ran. Skirting the dense, thorny bush they found a grey-haired man slumped in a heap, a bloody tourniquet tied round one of his legs and dark red stains visible underneath his leather jerkin. How he'd managed to keep firing, and with such deadly accuracy, with wounds that bad Haden had no idea

'Decker, quick, bring the water!' Haden knelt down by the man. 'Who are you?'

'Rafus,' the man whispered, blood dribbling down his chin, 'Rafus Ka'Var, out of Quadrine . . .'

Haden was no doctor, but it didn't take one of those to know that this man was in a bad way. Very bad. He was going to die, and there was nothing Haden could do to stop it, but at least he could make this stranger's last few hours as comfortable as possible.

5   Last Words

'Where's Quadrine?' Haden asked; he'd sent Decker off to try and find this man, Rafus's, horse and the two Sardar mounts, while he set about getting him into some shade.

'A long way from here, boy. A long way . . .' Rafus grunted with obvious pain as Haden hauled him none-too-gently up against the trunk of a small, wizened tree. 'And I am not going to see it again, I know that, so you don't have to try and hide anything from me. And don't waste too much of your food or water – or sympathy, for that matter – on me. My luck finally ran out, as luck always has to.'

'My father used to say that you only had so much luck and that it was an unreliable friend. You never knew if it would be there when you really needed it.'

'He sounds like a wise man.'

'He knew a lot . . .' Haden looked away, not wanting this stranger to see how much he missed his father. 'What were you doing out here?'

'I was looking for someone, who I'll never find now. You two?'

'We found the people *we* were looking for.'

'Them?' Rafus nodded over towards the dark tower of rock. 'Why?'

Haden bent down and picked up one of the marauder's pistols and pointed it out at the horizon.

'They killed everyone. All my family and every single person in the village. They set fire to our homes and now there's nothing left. I wanted to kill them.'

'You got one.'

'Yes . . .' Haden lowered the gun. 'I got one.'

'Three people destroyed your whole settlement?'

Haden shook his head. 'There were a lot more, but they split up and we followed the smaller group. My father always said divide . . .'

' . . . and conquer?' Rafus interrupted. 'Who was your father?'

'Akatine . . . he was Sten Akatine.'

Rafus stiffened, a confused look crossing his face. For a moment Haden thought the man's time had come and he was going to die right there and then. 'Are you . . . ?'

Rafus shook his head and coughed, spitting blood onto the ground.

'You're Akatine's son?' Haden nodded and Rafus smiled, shaking his head again. 'You can never second-guess the Fates. Never.'

'What d'you mean?'

'It was your father I was looking for.'

'*My* father?' Way out in the scrubland Haden could see Decker had managed to catch all three horses and was bringing them back in. 'Why? He was just a blacksmith.'

'For as long as *you'd* known him, maybe. But he was rather more than that, a legend, in his own way. In his own business.'

'What business?'

Rafus glanced at this boy who had appeared out of nowhere, not quite in time to save his life. To look at there was a lot of his father about him and the old man wondered why Akatine hadn't told his son anything about who he was and what he'd been. He also wondered how much, if any, of Akatine's fearsome spirit and steely nerve the boy had.

'He was a soldier,' Rafus finally replied. 'So I suppose you could say his business was war.'

'I don't believe you!' Haden had never wanted the stories told behind his father's back to be true, especially the ones about how many people he'd killed.

'No reason you should, boy, no reason at all. It's true, nonetheless. Why else would I traipse all the way across this forsaken wasteland if he was *just* a simple blacksmith? I did it because I needed his help, badly.

And now you tell me that, even if I wasn't dying, I'd be too late. I've failed . . .'

'What were you trying to do?'

'Stop a terrible thing from happening.'

'And how could my father have helped you?'

'Did your father tell you *nothing* about the old days?'

Haden shook his head.

'He was a truly gifted strategist, and fought like a chess player, always at least two, three moves ahead . . . I don't think he knew the meaning of the word defeat. He may have turned his back on his past to go home and start a family but, like you said, he knew a lot and I needed his help.' Rafus winced as he moved himself into a more comfortable position. 'Whether he'd have given it to me, I don't know, but I had to ask. Unfortunately, somehow the Sardar knew I was on my way, and those three were out here looking for me.'

'Why?'

'You may well find this hard to believe, seeing me now, but I am . . . I *was* a powerful man.' Rafus saw the look of disbelief that Haden tried unsuccessfully to hide. 'Did your father ever tell you that knowledge was power, something like that?'

'Yes,' Haden nodded.

'Well he was right, but knowledge can be a dangerous thing too: not enough and you can make the wrong decisions; too much about the wrong people and you can end up like me.'

'And you know something about the Sardar?'

'Your father and I always had our suspicions,' Rafus shivered, even though it wasn't at all cold. 'For years, decades, we've all treated the Sardar as a nuisance – a vicious nuisance, admittedly, but one the Territories have seen fit to put off doing anything about. Akatine always said it would lead to trouble . . .' Rafus spotted Decker, now only a couple of hundred yards away, leading the three horses. 'He may be dumb, your friend, but he isn't stupid.'

Haden knew this was true, but right then he didn't want to be reminded of how badly he and his friends had treated Decker.

'What's the trouble my father was talking about?'

'We've let the Sardar get too strong . . . far too strong. And we're all to blame, all the Territories, Sektaine, Cherinna and Uskarnha – the bigger ones, like Messanine and Quadrine, where I come from, even had "peace treaties" with the Sardar leader, Dasmed Usshien. We actually gave him the latest weaponry to "assist" with keeping the eastern borders intact and "safe" from outside attack. Looking back I can't believe how stupid we've been.'

Haden shrugged and looked away. Truthfully he had no idea what Rafus was talking about and suspected he might be rambling, which was a bad sign. His father had never said anything about 'the old days', and in Starpoint, so insignificant and far from anywhere, no one cared what was happening elsewhere in the world. Other places had little or no meaning. Until the Sardar had decided to pay a visit.

'They came to kill your father, you know.'

Haden whirled round, mouth agape.

'It wasn't a random attack, I'm pretty sure of it. He had a fearsome reputation, Akatine, and they must've found out that's where he was and they came to get him.'

'But – but why kill everyone else?'

'Because they could,' Rafus sighed, which turned into a rasping cough. 'The Sardar are animals, and through our own stupidity we've allowed ourselves to think that we had them on a leash . . . that we could control them and make them do our bidding. But we were wrong, and now they're well on their way to being able to take control of whatever they want.'

'I don't understand! I don't understand *any*thing . . .' Haden watched as Decker tethered the horses to a nearby tree, then took the saddlebags off the jittery piebald one. He glanced back at Rafus and saw that his eyelids were fluttering, his forehead creased with frown of discomfort.

'D'you want to sleep for a bit, tell me the rest later?'

Rafus's eyes snapped open. 'I don't have any "later", boy, and precious little "now" left. Sit down and listen.' He looked up at Decker, looming over him. 'And you. Both of you listen to me, and after I've finished, I'll have one question to ask you.'

Decker put the saddlebags down and came to sit cross-legged next to Haden, as if he was back in the schoolroom and about to hear a story. It might've been comical if the man opposite them hadn't been in sight of Death's door.

'Something is going on with the Sardar; Usshien is definitely up to no good . . .' Rafus coughed again and gestured to Haden for a sip of water. 'I've known this for quite a while, but I had no absolute proof and no one would listen to me – in fact I was told that I was rocking the boat, and if I didn't shut up I would be sacked.'

'What's your job then?' Haden sat back down.

'I used to be Quadrine's Controller of Information, a spy, if you like.'

'Used to be?'

'I didn't shut up. But there are a few others who, like me, believe it's never a good thing to play with fire. We think the Territories, all of them, are about to get badly burned, but until we have evidence no one's going to listen to us. My biggest fear was that, even if I managed to get it, I would be too late, but I had to try. Your father was the only person I could trust . . . I have someone else working closely with me, already inside Sardar territory, and I needed the Akatine I used to know. The three of us, we could've had a chance, but now . . .'

Rafus doubled over, a bout of coughing shaking him like a puppet, and Haden leapt up.

'What can I do?'

Sitting back, his face pale flour and water, Rafus wiped his lips. 'Answer my question.'

Haden looked at Decker, who shrugged. 'What is it?'

'I was going to ask your father to come with me to Ghadra, the Sardar stronghold . . . to help me find out what Usshien is doing, what his plans are, and get the information back to Quadrine.'

'What if he'd said no?'

'I'd've begged and pleaded, offered bribes and called in the few favours Akatine still owed me.'

'You think he'd have gone with you, left us all behind?' Haden asked.

'I saved his life once –' Rafus hacked some blood up. '– he did owe me. He was my last chance, except . . .'

Haden waited for Rafus to finish, but he didn't.

'Except what?'

'Where I come from,' he said at last, his breathing shallow and ragged, 'a son takes on the debts of his father when he dies.'

Haden flicked a glance at Decker and saw his look of questioning surprise that mirrored exactly how he felt. How was he supposed to answer a comment like that? Where he came from the same was true, but how did he know this man, blood-soaked and staring Death in the face, wasn't lying about his father's obligations?

'Is it *so* much to ask?' There was an edge to Rafus's voice, a hint of desperation. 'You can take whatever I have – maps, notes, information, water, food, ammunition, money, everything. Because what have you got to go back to? The Sardar have left you with nothing. Nothing . . .'

Haden was at a loss for what to say. This man, who *said* he'd known his father, wanted him and Deck to go on what could only be a dangerous and probably suicidal journey, all to help people he'd never met who lived in a place he hadn't heard of . . .

'You could lie,' Rafus said, interrupting and echoing Haden's thoughts; he laughed, then started coughing again. 'I'd never know. I'll not be here much longer . . . a different sort of journey to take.'

'I . . . um . . .' Haden glanced at Decker, for whom he was going to have to speak. The other was sitting, shoulders hunched and with an oddly serious, thoughtful expression on his dirt-smeared face. A big part of Haden wanted nothing more to do with these Sardar. He'd done what he'd said he would – kill the first one he met with his father's dagger – and he didn't really feel any the better for it. Why should he go looking for more trouble?

'You don't have to answer, but you must promise me this . . . whatever you decide to do, before you leave, bury me deep enough so the vultures and the Rift dogs can't get me. I don't want my bones picked over by flea-ridden scavengers. And leave my boots on . . .'

' . . . because a man should be buried in his boots.' Haden looked away, biting his lip, and took a deep breath. 'My father used to say that . . .' he whispered.

'So he did.'

In the silence Haden heard the softest of sighs, then felt Decker touch his arm. He looked over at Rafus. The

44

man's eyes were closed and a thin trickle of blood was running slowly down his chin. He'd died, taking no answers with him and leaving Haden with a bitter, bitter taste in his mouth. Maybe he should have lied. It wouldn't have cost him anything.

The old man stood up and stretched; nowadays, if he stayed sitting down for too long, his joints started creaking like an old shed door. It was, along with forgetting things, one of the worst aspects of not being young any more.

'Why did he have to die, Grampa?'

'Do you mean, could I tell things a different way so he didn't?' The boy nodded. ''Fraid not, son. I may tell you a lot of stories, but I never tell you any lies. That's the way it happened and nothing can change it.'

'So the Sardar were really, really bad?'

'They were.'

'Are they still around today?'

'Sure.' The boy's face dropped. 'But they don't go round killing people any more.'

'Why, what happened?'

'Everything changes . . . nothing stays the same. You want to hear the rest of the story?'

The boy nodded.

'Fine. Well, what we have to do now is leave Haden and Decker to the rest of their journey through the Rift . . .'

'Did they bury Rafus, like he wanted them to?'

'Of course, it was the least they could do.'

'And do they go to that place, Ghadra, like Rafus asked?'

'You'll have to wait and see – that's the whole point of a story, waiting to see . . . you want anything else to drink?'

'No thanks, Grampa.'

'If it's all right by you I'll stay on my feet for a bit.'

The boy shrugged and smiled.

'So,' the old man stretched his arms out, 'once they'd buried Rafus, and piled some stones on top to mark the grave and keep the scavengers out, Haden and Decker opened up the saddlebags and went through what was in them. And there was a lot. Along with half a dozen or more boxes of cartridges for the rifle, they found a number of beautifully printed linen maps, a hefty leather-bound journal filled with notes, sketches and diagrams, some bundled rolls of money in various currencies . . . and two pouches, each containing at least fifty decimas in gold coin.'

The old man stopped walking and looked down at the boy.

'And back then, son, you could buy a house with fifty decimas of gold, or live like a king for a year, whichever you wanted to do . . . it was a lot of money.'

'And they took it all?'

'Rafus gave it to them, remember?'

'Right . . .'

'These were honest Outlander boys, Mykel. They could've taken off with everything and never looked back. But they didn't. They sat down and Haden read through Rafus's notebook, every page . . .'

'Haden could read?'

'He might've been a blacksmith's son, but he'd had an education, of sorts.'

'What about Decker?'

'Decker? He was a very good listener . . .'

'What did they find out?'

'They found out all about a man called Pero Esquabar . . .'

6 IN THE LION'S DEN

PERO ESQUABAR WASN'T THE kind of man who took advice, or was ever in any doubt that he was right. At least that was the impression he liked to give. But at that moment, in this large, windowless room – lit, at whatever time you came into it, by lamps and candles, smelling of tallow, sweat and fear – he was beginning to wonder if coming to the Sardar stronghold of Ghadra had been *such* a good idea after all.

He'd assumed (in his head he could hear his own words coming back to him 'Never, *ever*, assume *any*thing!') that Dasmed Usshien's almost pathological need to dominate would make him as easy to lead as a sheep. And, for a while at least, this had proved to be true. Promises of an ultimate weapon that would give the man power over any Territory he wanted had meant that Usshien had provided everything that had been asked for.

Unfortunately, the experiments hadn't *quite* gone as anticipated. Which was why Esquabar was now waiting in this room somewhere inside Usshien's maze of a house. The sciencer looked around him. The word 'house' hardly described the massive rambling labyrinth of buildings in the eastern part of the city that made up Usshien's living quarters and was the centre of his operations.

In the distance Esquabar heard the sharp clatter of metal-heeled boots on flagstones and he knew that if he didn't have the right answers to whatever questions Usshien chose to throw at him, then he would probably be a dead man before very long. The Sardar had never been known for the quality of their mercy and if there was one thing Dasmed Usshien hated it was failure.

Pacing up and down, Esquabar bit his nails and began to wish he'd never heard of this remote, inhospitable city, built high up on a plateau in the Karpak Mountains. That he'd never been tempted to hoodwink a man rumoured to have killed two of his own sons out of spite because they looked like their mother. Just *what* had he been thinking?

'Do you take me for an imbecile?'

A pair of heavy double doors had slammed open, thundering against the walls and making every flame

49

in the room quake, announcing that Dasmed Usshien was entering the room. What the man lacked in height he made up for with a poisonous disposition and a hair-trigger temper. He walked around Esquabar, inspecting him as if he were some bedraggled goat up for sale in a market.

'Well?' Usshien went and sat in the raised, throne-like chair that was the only piece of furniture in the dank, shadowy room and put his head on one side as he waited for an answer.

'I, uh . . .'

'The delivery that came yesterday?' Usshien interrupted, gesturing behind him. 'That was the last one. No more of that stinking rubbish – I want results, Esquabar. I want the weapon you promised me. And I want to see it soon. Very soon.'

'But . . .'

'You've had everything you said you needed: manpower, materials, time . . . and my trust. Which I am beginning to feel that you have abused.'

'We have had problems –'

'I *know* you've had problems.' Usshien leant forward, smiling, candlelight glinting off his array of gold teeth and his dark, oiled hair. 'Six of my men have died because of your "problems", Esquabar, and I am running out of patience! You said this would all be ready in a matter of months, that come summer everything would be finished and I could start launching attacks.' He sat back and a look of bemusement swept across his face as he spread his hands out. 'But do you see me attacking?'

'I am *very* nearly there, sir . . .' Esquabar swallowed, a bitter taste in his mouth. He hated toadying to people like Dasmed Usshien, but he was *so* close to succeeding that he knew he would actually lick the man's boots if he had to. 'A month, no more, that's all I need.'

'You've got a week.' Usshien stood. 'Seven days from tomorrow and you will show me this weapon and it will work. They found a spy snooping around the smelting works a couple of days ago and I think the Territories are beginning to have their suspicions. So it *will* work.'

'Really? A spy!' Esquabar's feelings of guilt, combined with his paranoia that he might at any moment be caught, had made him extremely jumpy. 'What, um, happened to them?'

'As it appears I am surrounded by incompetents and cretins, the spy escaped.'

'Oh.'

Cracking his knuckles loudly, Usshien marched out, leaving Pero Esquabar alone again in the twilit room. He looked around, finding it hard to believe that outside the sun was shining. Even this stinking city looked less disgusting on such a morning, like it had when he'd first arrived in Ghadra. He sighed deeply. Much as he would have preferred it to be otherwise, he had no one to blame but himself for the predicament in which he now found himself. A thought that served only to make him feel worse.

'A *week*!' Esquabar muttered as he sloped out of the room, chewing his lip. 'What on *earth* can I do in a week?'

As soon as he got out of the Sardar leader's dark, maze-like headquarters, Pero Esquabar made a beeline for the building that Dasmed Usshien had given him to live and work in. It was three storeys high and had a cavernous basement, and there, waiting for his return and news of the meeting, would be his assistant, Mowler.

Mowler was the only other person in the whole world who knew what the plan was. The boy was his sister's oldest son and, since he had to trust someone with the knowledge that he was trying to cheat Dasmed Usshien, Esquabar had supposed that a family member was a better choice than many he could have made. Added to which, Mowler was actually very clever – something of a surprise, considering what dull beasts both his parents were.

Esquabar was a sciencer. He believed in logical thought, systematic observation, structured knowledge. He did not believe in magic. He had spent his entire life seeking to understand how the world *really* worked, to be an expert, to comprehend, to know the truth. Not chase ridiculous ideas, myths and fantasies.

So he had dismissed his chance discovery as a mistake. It was, after all, ridiculously implausible.

Correction: it was impossible. No one could turn lead into gold, or coal into diamonds. *That* was transmutation. Or magic, if you will. And it did *not* happen except in stories.

But there wasn't a single hole in *any* of his calculations, and he had gone over them with the finest of fine-toothed combs again and again until, eventually, there had been no denying the results: he *could* turn lead into gold! His only problems, and they were undeniably big ones, were keeping what he'd discovered a secret and, moreover, getting his hands on the huge sums of money he'd need to enable him to put his calculations into practice. And that was where Dasmed Usshien came into the equation.

Esquabar pulled the bell cord next to the smaller entrance set into the building's tall double doors. Today's code was: once, twice; pause; once, twice and wait. A few moments later he saw a shadow pass over the spyhole he'd had Mowler put in, then he heard locks being turned and bolts thrown.

'I was beginning to worry, uncle,' Mowler said as he opened the door just enough to let Esquabar in. 'What happened?'

'He kept me waiting longer than he usually does.'

'Is everything all right?'

'Yes, and, ah, no . . .' Esquabar motioned for Mowler to go down the stairs. 'As you can see, I'm not dead, or missing any limbs, but he wants to see the weapon – and see it working – seven days from tomorrow.'

'Seven *days*? Seven weeks would be pushing it!'

'Don't exaggerate, boy.'

'But – but –' Mowler's face was a picture of disbelief. 'We're nowhere *near* a complete solution to the stability problems – *and* that last load of dacrylith they brought in from Massenine was short by a couple of hundredweight.'

Esquabar walked over to the huge bunkers where they stored the oily-black shale commonly known as slack but more properly as dacrylith.

'Usshien told me this lot's the last we're going to get until he sees something.' He put on a pair of thick leather gloves and picked up a piece of the rock, which looked like it was covered in a dark, glutinous syrup. 'Hard to believe what we can make out of this stuff, eh, Mowler?'

Mowler didn't find it at all hard to believe. He'd been with his uncle, traipsing all over the Massenine wastelands for months, camping out in the middle of nowhere while they poked about in the millions of tons of dacrylith just lying there, waiting for someone to work out what use it might be.

This had been yet another of the many get-rich-quick schemes that his uncle had devised, but one of the few which had actually come up with the goods. The goods being a clear, dangerously unpredictable and highly flammable liquid, which the oily-black rock produced after a series of complex distillations. Mowler had even made up the name for it. Originally he'd called it

Dacryphyre, but now he and his uncle simply called it Phyre. It seemed to suit the volatile nature of the substance so much better.

It was not long after he'd created the first samples of Phyre that Mowler's uncle had chanced upon the transmutation process. Almost overnight he had become a man obsessed, putting everything else aside until he'd worked out a scheme for getting the funds he needed to pursue his dream of creating unimaginable wealth from base metal and common-or-garden minerals. Although quite why he'd *ever* thought it was a good idea to promise a maniac like Usshien access to the most powerful explosive in the world he didn't know. For a clever man, his uncle wasn't always very wise.

'What's Usshien going to do to us when he finds out that the weapon doesn't work, *probably* because we've secretly been using his money and resources to work on something else?' Mowler's shoulders slumped. 'My mum's going to be very upset if he kills me.'

'Don't worry about your mother, she'll . . .'

'It's not my *mother* I'm worried about!' Mowler interrupted. '*She's* not the one going to meet a hideous end, slaughtered like a goat.'

'He won't do that.'

'He will.' Mowler's shoulders slumped even further in a resigned shrug. 'He kills people for looking at him the wrong way, so when he finds what *we've* been up to . . . What are we going to *do*, uncle? I don't want to die.'

'Neither do I, so we'll *both* have to hope that the idea
I had on the way back here works . . .'

7 THE JOURNEY STARTS

HADEN FELT STRANGE. SLIGHTLY uncomfortable. It wasn't just the fact that he was sitting in a finely crafted leather saddle on a beautiful roan mare, more that he felt that he'd in some way assumed another man's life. Not only was he riding Rafus's horse and wearing items of his clothing, he'd taken on the man's mission as well. Up until yesterday he'd not had the vaguest notion of where Quadrine was and now he and Decker were about to put their lives at risk for the place.

After reading all the way through the journal with its copious notes in small, neat, spidery handwriting, he now knew everything Rafus had discovered about what the Sardar were doing. But not *why* they were doing it. It was obvious from the number of pages with underlined questions on them that while Rafus had found out that something was going on, he hadn't the slightest idea what all the information he'd gathered meant.

Why had the Sardar started taking prisoners when 'No prisoners!' had always been their battle cry and motto? Why were they using these prisoners as slave labour to dig up and transport large amounts of apparently useless dacrylith shale from Massenine? Who was this mysterious person, Pero Esquabar, who was rumoured to be behind what was going on? What was the mysterious substance he was supposed to have discovered? And what did it all mean for the Territories? A few of Rafus's journal entries had referred to someone called Blade, whom Haden worked out was the person already in the Sardar Territory. This Blade person would know what to do – what Rafus would want *them* to do – but possibly the most troubling question was how were they ever going to find each other?

Haden had no idea what the answers to any of these questions were, although he did know that if Rafus hadn't been an old friend of his father's they wouldn't be setting off into the unknown. With what they'd taken from the Sardar corpses and what Rafus had had with him, they would have been very well set up and could've gone on their way to anywhere they liked. But instead, here they were, heading for Ghadra.

As he rode, Haden mulled over these thoughts then he fell to thinking about his father, about the man whose position he'd inherited by taking on this quest. He'd been, to be truthful, an odd mixture of a man: funny but strict; tough yet sentimental. He was a man people trusted but who himself had few close friends. And there was obviously a side to him that he'd kept entirely private, so private Haden wouldn't have been surprised if even his mother hadn't known about it. He wondered whether his father would have gone with Rafus Ka'var, the man from Quadrine; in the end deciding that he would, and that *he*, Haden, was only doing what his father would've done. Had Akatine not been butchered by the Sardar.

Haden looked over at Decker, riding next to him on the Sardar mount they'd kept. He looked the happiest Haden could ever remember seeing him. 'OK, Deck?'

Decker grinned back, patting the horse's neck, then pulled a hefty revolver out of the holster he was now wearing and grinned even wider. Haden knew how he felt. Strapped to his horse was Rafus's rifle. It belonged to him now and it was odd knowing that he owned this beautiful, deadly thing. With its dark, polished-wood stock and oiled magazine and barrel, it had the elegance of a machine made to do two things very well: protect and kill. Haden had never owned a gun before but now he had this rifle and, like Decker, two pistols, they'd certainly get some respect in the next place they visited. Although where the pair were headed, he had a notion respect was the last thing they'd need, nor was it what they were looking for.

'First chance we get, Deck, we'll buy ourselves some new clothes,' he looked down at what he was wearing, the threadbare and dirty garments a constant reminder of where they'd come from and what had occurred there. 'Don't think I've *ever* worn anything new in my whole life.' Decker nodded in agreement.

'About time, eh?'

In reply, Decker kicked his horse into a canter and beckoned Haden to follow.

They'd spent the night camped in a copse by a small stream. Decker, who appeared to have an eagle's eyes, had spotted some plains deer and Haden had surprised himself by hitting one with his first shot (surprised also by how the rifle had kicked like a mule and bruised his shoulder). After eating better than they had for days, the two of them had fallen asleep under a night sky, dust-spattered with stars, wrapped in blankets and using their saddles for pillows.

Haden wasn't sure at first what had dragged him unwillingly out of a dream and into the early dawn. Then he heard the spooked, high-pitched whinny of the horses and knew that there was someone else nearby. Grabbing the rifle, which he'd slept with under his blanket, he sat up blinking the sleep from his eyes as he tried to see what had frightened the animals.

The first thing he noticed was that Decker wasn't anywhere to be seen, his friend's blanket was in a crumpled heap next to him. And then he noticed a slight, silhouetted figure of a man walking away from where the horses were tethered. The rising sun was right in front of the man, flaring around his head and making it look like he was on fire.

'Who are you?' Haden pushed himself up and chambered a round in the rifle. 'What've you done to Deck?'

The man, a soft breeze playing with his ragged clothing, didn't reply, just turned his hands outwards and looked over at Haden.

'Well?' Something about the man made Haden nervous, even though *he* was the one with the gun. Maybe it was the fact that even though his face was in deep shadow, he could see his teeth and the whites of his eyes as he smiled at him. Then, in a blur, the man waved one of his hands and a cluster of small birds burst from nowhere into the air and flew over to one of the trees.

'My name is Eloi the Keeper and you have violated a *holy place* . . .' the man hissed. 'This is *sacred* ground. You have disturbed the spirits. They will want you *punished*!'

Haden was beginning to wonder if he wasn't still asleep and dreaming – birds appearing out of nowhere? Holy places? Then the man waved his other hand and a red scarf appeared in it.

'But will they want you punished with silk,' Eloi said, shaking the scarf, 'or with wood?' In a flourish the length of red silk had somehow turned into a gnarled wooden cane, which the man grabbed with both hands and took up an angular attack position. He could have looked ridiculous but he didn't. He looked serious and threatening.

Haden stood his ground. Could this person, whoever or whatever he was, have made Decker vanish the same way he'd made birds appear and silk turn into a stick? A part of him, the part that remembered the fables and stories he'd been told as a child, wanted to take a step back.

'Tell me what you want.' Haden did move, but sideways so that the sun wasn't directly behind the man and he could see him better.

'Or what?'

'Or I'll shoot you.' Haden cocked the rifle, the click loud in the morning silence. He could now make out that the man was quite old, his grey hair tied in hundreds of thin plaits, each with a coloured ribbon running through it so it looked like his head was alive with tiny snakes. The man wasn't dressed in rags, as he'd first thought, but ragged animal skins and, as the old man's head turned Haden could see shiny, coal-black pebble eyes set close to a sharp beak of a nose, following him.

'What d'you want?'

'Recompense.' Eloi smiled, revealing a snaggle of brown teeth, and took a step towards Haden, who held his position. 'You should make amends. This is a hallowed place, couldn't you tell? Did they teach you *nothing* where you come from?'

'You don't know *any*thing about where I come from!' Haden could feel a cold anger rising from the pit of his stomach, pushing back his fear of the unknown and his growing worries about what had happened to Decker. 'Take your tricks and your tales and go away . . .'

In front of him the skinny, spare-framed figure span the wooden cane into a blur, clapped his hands together . . . and the cane disappeared.

'It's gone.' Eloi opened his hands, letting a coarse brown powder fall to the ground. 'Dust to dust. I could do that to you, boy.' He shook his hands clean. 'Show me any more disrespect, and I will.'

A quiet voice whispered *What if it's true?* in Haden's head at the same time as he felt his finger tighten on the rifle's trigger. He took a deep breath.

'You'll have to catch a bullet first.'

Eloi's beady eyes twitched, his smile froze for a moment, then quickly thawed. 'You have so much, you and your friend – whom I have done no harm to, my word of honour, may the spirits strike me down,' Eloi bowed his head slightly, 'and I have nothing.'

He gestured, head on one side, at the shabby skins he was wearing.

Having so recently had everything taken away from him, Haden now knew what it was like to have nothing. But he didn't believe this Eloi was a true enchanter or a wizard, or, he realised, that he'd really done anything to Decker. Although it *was* very odd that he was nowhere to be seen . . .

With all these conflicting, confusing thoughts rattling round his head like dice in a cup, Haden didn't know what to do next.

'A small gift?' Eloi, holding the index finger and thumb of his left hand an inch apart, raised his eyebrows. 'For the spirits?'

Holding the rifle in the crook of his arm, Haden dug in one of his pockets and pulled out a leather pouch into which he'd put some of Rafus's gold coins. He threw a couple of half-quarter decimas on the ground. 'Buy them a drink.'

Almost too fast to see, Eloi retrieved the two gold coins from the ground and he stood for a moment, examining them as they lay on the palm of his hand.

'Most generous . . .'

'My mother always said "Remember the poor, and if *you* are ever poor, *you* will be remembered".'

'A wise woman.'

'She was.'

Eloi carefully put the coins away, turned on his heels and, out of nowhere, had the wooden cane back in his right hand.

'Until the next time,' he said over his shoulder as he walked off.

'I doubt we'll be coming back this way.'

'Goodbye, then . . .'

Haden watched Eloi the Keeper walk away through the copse, noticing a spring in his step that made him look a bit like a child, happy with the gift that had been given. Shaking his head Haden turned to go and look for Decker, which was when he spotted the half-empty goat's skin water carriers. He picked them up thinking that he could kill two birds with one stone by filling them and checking along the stream at the same time.

He'd just finished replenishing their water supplies when he heard a noise and looked up to see Decker coming from downstream. There was something different about him and for a moment Haden couldn't work out what it was. Then he realised: Decker was clean, and soaked to the skin.

'Been swimming, Deck?'

Decker shook his head holding up a bag he had slung over his shoulder with one hand and making a sideways, wavy motion with the other.

'You caught a fish?'

Decker held up two fingers.

'With your bare *hands*?' All thoughts of the strange man, with his odd talk of spirits and holy places, disappeared as he saw Decker nod gleefully, a huge grin splitting his face.

'You're full of surprises, Deck – let's get that fire going again!'

 **8**   SEEING THINGS

IT WAS STILL EARLY when they left their makeshift campsite, following a route Rafus had marked on one of the maps – out of the Rift into wide, partially forested prairie. The only thing of any real interest looked to be at least two days' ride away: a city called Jardesh.

Haden had never been to a city before, and this was too good a chance to pass up – even with the slightly odd note in Rafus's journal, a note with the word 'avoid', underlined twice, but with a question mark by it. Yes or no? Find an alternative route, or go?

'Jardesh,' Haden took a sip of water. He liked the sound of the word. 'Our first city, eh, Deck?'

•

It took a while for Haden to realise that something was happening. At first he took no notice of the slight buzzing in his ears, but then he became aware that strange, half hidden *things* had started sneaking into the borderline of his vision and the buzzing had turned into whispers. Voices. And the tips of his fingers had gone numb.

Then, quite slowly, the nightmare began.

Bit by tiny bit, reality slipped away to be replaced by a growing blizzard of images and a swelling howl of sound. Column after column of ants, weaving into the air like the huge, frantic tendrils of some insane plant, appeared from out of the ground. Trees and bushes burst into flames and, sitting on their branches, small fanged creatures with eyes like red coals grabbed at him and called out his name.

Engulfed by such unspeakable horror, Haden felt a tidal wave of fear rising up. As he tried and failed to stay on his horse (an animal that was melting beneath him in the heat of the scorched landscape) he saw Decker . . . or something that *looked* like Decker. A voice rattled around Haden's skull screaming that this was not Decker, that it was an imposter. And a single thought came rushing into his head savagely pushing every other one away: kill this thing!

Trying to ignore the fact that the ground was pulling at his feet and attempting to swallow him, Haden pulled his father's dagger from its sheath and waded through the clawing earth towards the Decker-creature, which was kneeling on the ground and had luminous green tears streaming down its cheeks. A rainbow halo of coloured light began glowing all around it, and as Haden watched – fascinated, despite the fact that he knew he *must* annihilate this monster – he became aware of something moving towards him through the incandescent trees.

It was a man. A wild man, his hair alive with whip-thin coloured snakes, brandishing an axe. It was someone he felt he ought to recognise, but couldn't quite work out why. As he stared at this man careening towards him, his teeth bared and axe raised, a name crawled out from somewhere in his head and shouted at him. *Eloi!* it said. *It's Eloi!*

Eloi the Keeper . . . but what was *he* doing in this terrible place? And *why* was he running at him with an axe, shouting that he must die? As Haden stopped and turned to concentrate on this new and somehow more real menace he became aware that the misery and torment all around him was fading away at the edges, the terrors losing their strength and power. And as the horrors ebbed away he realised that he could hear something else, apart from Eloi's threats . . . a strange, almost childlike wailing.

Crouched, like an animal at bay, Haden risked a glance to his right, from where the sound came. There, crawling on the ground, he saw Decker, face covered in real tears, mouth open. It was Decker. Mute, silent Deck was crying. Out loud.

With astonishment fighting to replace panic, and reality sliding jerkily back into place, Haden turned to face Eloi. He dropped the dagger and drew his revolver out of its holster. The ragged, axe-wielding figure stumbled to a halt some ten, twelve yards away, and squinted at him, his mouth twitching.

'Oh. Drat . . .'

'You *knew* there'd be a next time, that we'd meet again, didn't you!' Haden cocked the pistol's knurled hammer as the death throes of the nightmare skittered away, and it dawned on him the monstrous hallucinations had something to do with this skinny old man.

'Ah,' Eloi, slowly brought the axe down behind his back, 'yes.'

'But how –' Before Haden could finish his question, Eloi had spun round and was haring away, his multicoloured plaits flying behind him. Raising his pistol Haden fired a shot over Eloi's shoulder.

'The next one won't miss!' he shouted.

Eloi skidded to a halt like he was attached to an invisible rope and Haden walked towards him, not at all sure what he was going to do next. When he got close enough he grabbed Eloi's shoulder and swung him round, the pistol barrel inches from his chest.

'Talk, old man.'

'Don't hurt me . . .' Eloi cringed, his voice was whiny and scared.

'Hurt you? *You* were the one coming at *me* with an axe!'

'I was just trying to frighten you, make sure you and your friend would run away so I could steal your things. That's all.'

'That's *all*?' The memory of the awful sights and sounds he'd just witnessed – the chittering creatures, the fires, the clawing earth – still crawled in the back of his mind and behind him he could hear Decker's weird, anguished moaning. 'You did that – you made me see all those *things* – how?'

'What things?' Eloi's attempt at an innocent face was a complete failure. Haden jabbed the gun at him. 'Yes . . . um, *those* things . . . I, ah, I put something, a little powder, in your water carriers. It makes you see what isn't really there.'

'Where did you get it from?'

'I make it, from plants,' Eloi took a small step backwards, away from the gun barrel. 'It's a hard life out here, and this is how I get what I need. Maybe I, ah, put a little *too* much in this time –' he shrugged, palms upwards, '– sorry?'

'My friend,' Haden nodded back at Decker. 'What happened to him?'

'How d'you mean?'

'He's a mute, or at least he *was* a mute, till he drank some of your potion. How did that happen?'

'No idea. On my life, I don't know how that would happen. What, um, what might you be intending to do with me – are you going to shoot me?' Eloi danced a tiny, nervous dance from one foot to the other, cursing himself for not claiming at least *some* responsibility for this seemingly miraculous 'cure'.

'I ought to . . .' Haden glanced at Decker, still sitting on the ground, a look of total and utter bewilderment on his face. 'But I won't.'

Eloi mistakenly took this to mean he could make himself scare, then felt the gun in his ribs.

'You stay right where you are!'

'Right – right where I am. Of course, certainly . . .'

'D'you have that powder with you?' Haden put his hand out and made a beckoning gesture.

'The powder?' Haden nodded and Eloi's fingers tripped over themselves to untie a small, black leather pouch hanging from his belt. 'It's yours.'

Haden was about to untie the pouch and pour the powder away when he stopped, muttered, 'You never know . . .' to himself and pocketed it. Then he flicked a small silver coin at Eloi.

'A fair exchange?' he said.

Eloi snatched at the coin and missed. 'Generous, I'd say, but . . . ?' He raised his eyebrows questioningly as he bent to pick it up.

'Why?' said Haden. 'Because I was taught to pay what I owe, and anyway, what good would it do me to hurt you?'

Eloi frowned and shook his head. 'You are a strange young man.'

'This is a strange world, Eloi, as I've learnt every day since I left Starpoint.'

'Where's that?'

'Nowhere . . . not any more.' Haden went over to Decker, waving the pistol at Eloi. 'Now go, before I change my mind.'

As Eloi, glancing over his shoulder every few seconds, hurried away, Haden knelt down by Decker.

'You all right?'

'Wha'appen?' Decker's voice was slurred, like he'd been at the beer cask, and had a deep, slightly rasping tone to it.

'Dunno, Deck. Can you stand up?'

'I can *tor*!' Decker shouted, clambering unsteadily to his feet. 'I can spee . . . wiv my *mowf*! Howdi'appen? An why'd I see ni'mare . . . awake? Who tha' man?'

'No one . . .' Distracted by Decker's fishing exploits, it had slipped Haden's mind to say anything about his early morning encounter with Eloi. 'We both drank something. It was in the water and it made us see all those things – nightmares, like you said. And *somehow*, whatever was in the water's made you able to speak.'

'Magic . . . magic, magic, *magic*!' Decker grinned, one hand feeling his throat, the other touching his lips as he spoke, listening with obvious amazement and delight to his own voice. 'Mus' be.'

9 THE SILENT CITY

THE JOURNEY TO JARDESH took a solid day's riding, hours during which Haden got hardly a word in edgewise now that Decker had found his voice. Over the course of their journey, constant practise turned his slurred and garbled attempts to copy what he'd only ever been able to hear into a non-stop avalanche of words. A lifetime of trapped thoughts, feelings and opinions flowed out and Decker was, Haden thought, like a child with a new toy.

Watching Decker made him feel happy and sad at the same time; his delight at now having someone to talk to was tempered by the knowledge of how everyone – himself included – had looked down on Decker and treated him as simple-minded and foolish just because he couldn't talk. Now the words were free to be spoken, it was obvious how wrong they'd all been.

'Not far now, Haden.' Decker, who had Rafus's map, pointed ahead to the top of the rolling hill they would soon be cresting. 'Far as I can tell, it's off to the east in the next valley. We'll see it soon, wonder what it looks like? Never seen a city – d'you think it'll look like Starpoint, 'cept much bigger? Or will it be completely different? Probably we won't be able to tell from where we are . . . have to wait till we get closer, tomorrow. You said there'd be a wall round it, didn't you, I remember that. But you didn't say why. Why would they have a wall, Haden? To keep people out or to keep them in? Or is it both, like the fences round the animals – keep the wolves out and the sheep in. Maybe that's it . . .'

On it went, hour after hour of comments, questions, observations; Haden happy to let Decker talk as much as he liked. After all, he had a lot of catching up to do.

When Jardesh finally came into view the sight was enough to stop the flood of words. The place was the biggest man-made construction either of them had ever seen, far bigger than they had imagined it. The city, dark against the patchworked green plain in which it was set, was circled by a high, crenellated wall that had at least two massive gates that they could see. The last of the sun made the city glow a deep orange, like a huge ember that had fallen from some impossibly colossal fire. It looked beautiful and exotic and quite unlike anything Haden had ever seen before.

'Tomorrow . . .' he said.

'What?'

'We'll go in tomorrow, find out what a city's like – all those people!' Haden glanced over at Decker and saw he was frowning. 'What's the matter, Deck?'

'Don't know . . . doesn't look right.'

'What's a city s'*posed* to look like then? Considering we've neither of us ever been to one?'

'It doesn't look alive.'

Haden looked back at Jardesh and saw that Decker was right. 'You mean there'd be lights, right? And smoke from fires too . . .'

With dark falling fast, Haden realised he should be able to see the star-like glitter of lamp-light; he remembered even their speck of a village had twinkled in the distance in the black of an Outland night when he and his father had been coming home from a hunting trip. At the very least there should be torches at the gates yet there were none. Haden felt an involuntary shiver run down his back. Maybe it would all look different in the morning . . .

As they rode through the lush countryside the silence followed them like a wolf. Either side of the wide roadway there were signs everywhere that something was wrong: fields were untended, animals ill-cared for and there wasn't a sign of the people who should have been doing all the work.

They came to a halt after riding down a long avenue, through a tunnel of trees. Now they were some two or three hundred yards from one of the city's gates and as he brought his horse to a stop, Haden felt as if he was looking at a picture. Nothing moved.

He'd expected noise, bustle, toing and froing. Like Starpoint on market day, only a hundred, a *thousand* times more so. In his mind's eye he'd already seen the crowds, all dressed in wildly colourful clothing; he'd heard the tremendous din they made and smelt the baking bread and brewing ale. But ahead all he could see were the half-open doors in a gateway that was taller than any building he'd ever seen and beyond them, a weird stillness.

'Do we have to go in?'

Decker's question jolted Haden out of his thoughts.

'Say again?'

'You sure you want to go in? There'll be other cities, I can wait.'

'We're here . . . just a quick look, Deck? First sign of any trouble and we'll high-tail it, promise.'

Staring at the ground, Decker took a deep breath and nodded in silent agreement; he didn't want to go through these door and into this place, but he could see Haden *needed* to.

'We've got pistols and rifles, we'll be fine.' A small voice in Haden's head was whispering caution but, having come this far, he wasn't in the mood to listen to it. Instead, he spurred his horse on, kicking it into a trot.

Behind him he heard Decker follow suit.

As they neared the gates he could see the time-darkened wood was studded with iron spikes, with plenty of evidence that at some time in the city's history, it had fended off a good few attacks. The two sentry posts were empty and no one challenged them as they rode up to Jardesh. Haden reined in his horse and sat looking through the open doors. A wide, empty cobbled street stretched away with houses three, four storeys high on either side of it. The only thing moving was some rubbish being blown about in the breeze. He pulled his rifle out of its saddle holster, checked there was a bullet in the breach and slid it back in again.

'We'll be fine,' he said.

The sharp *klak* of the horses' hooves rang out loudly on the cobbled road echoing in the high, vaulted doorway, and then they were inside the city, riding up the long main street as small eddies of dust chased each other. The wind that had created them moaned and sighed and rattled ill-fitting windows. Haden tried to ignore his disappointment, but this was not how he'd pictured his first visit to a real city.

Narrow side streets and dark, cramped alleys ran off each side of the street and everywhere he looked, the vacant stare of empty windows returned his gaze. The emptiness was oppressive – no people, no cats, birds or dogs, no vermin even, just the death rattle of unlatched shutters.

There was, Haden knew, only one question that

needed answering: what had happened here? This place did not look like it had been attacked any time recently – no signs of battle, no evidence of pillaging – but whoever had lived here had left in something of a hurry. But who, or what, had caused a city of this size to be abandoned? Rafus had obviously known *something* wasn't quite right with this place, else why would he think it was probably a good place to avoid? But Haden had found no other details in his notebooks.

'No soul.'

Haden couldn't deny feeling jittery, and Decker's short, rather too accurate description of the place didn't help. He was just about to pull up his horse and admit that this whole thing had been a bad idea when the street curved round to the right, widened and gave out on to a vast, open space. Riding into it, Haden found himself in a square so big that he was sure you could fit the whole of Starpoint here. Whichever way he looked there were tall, balconied buildings with grand staircases leading up to their entrances, each one of a different design, each faced in coloured marble and decorated with delicately arched windows and gilded statues.

Haden was so amazed by the sights around him that he let his horse walk on and only stopped the mare when it seemed like he and Decker were almost at the centre of the square. He stood up in his stirrups, shielding his eyes, speechless with amazement.

'Something happened here.'

'Must've, Deck, for all the people to disappear . . .'

'No, look, over there.'

Haden turned round and saw what Decker was talking about. Behind him the frontage of one of the houses had been completely destroyed by an explosion. It looked as if the wall had been punched out from the inside, strewing masonry out into the square and he could see the exposed, fire-blackened innards of the building.

He was just about to say something when he was sure he heard someone calling out. *Was* it a voice he could hear echoing around the square?

'You hear that? Was it . . .'

'Yes.' Decker nodded, his ears sharper than Haden's. 'There's somebody left in this place.'

10 THE CITY WAKES

'CAN YOU SEE ANYTHING?' Haden reined back his horse, which appeared to have picked up some of his own nervousness and become skittish.

Decker shook his head. 'We should go.'

Wary after the run-in with Eloi, Haden unholstered his rifle and sat with it cradled in his arms.

'What if they're in trouble? Do we just leave them?'

Decker didn't answer.

And then, out of the corner of his eye, Haden saw something fluttering at a window in a building on the far side of the square. He dug into one of Rafus's satchels and brought out the leather case than held the man's brass binoculars. It took him a moment to find the open window and a few more to bring the image into focus.

'I thought I saw someone . . . it could've been a woman, but I can't hear what they're saying.'

'Help. Sounded like an old man, calling for help.'

'An old man?' Haden lowered the glasses. 'You can make that out?'

'Didn't have much else to do except listen, did I. Got good at it.'

'Can you hear anything else?' Haden slipped off the rifle's safety catch as he glanced nervously left and right.

'Nothing. What're we going to do?'

Haden pulled his horse to the right and urged it forward. 'Got to see what they want . . .'

'I don't like it.'

'I know, Deck.' Unbidden, from somewhere in his memory, Haden heard his father's voice, soft but clear: *in this life, you do as you would be done by, son*. It was the principle by which he'd lived and which he had drummed into his children. Haden knew that if he was abandoned in a place like this *he'd* want help and he wouldn't be able to forgive himself if he just rode away. 'I know . . .'

Stopping twenty or so yards from the building, Haden searched the façade for any more signs of who had called out, but there was nothing to be seen anywhere. He dismounted and started walking towards the building's magnificent double staircase.

'I'm coming with you.'

'Stay with the horses, Deck. Anything happens to them . . .' Haden didn't need to finish the sentence.

He walked up the steps and stood in front of the door, promising himself that at the first sign of danger he'd be gone. Considering what they'd seen of Jardesh so far whatever was in this building wasn't likely to be anything good. At the moment his imagination was racing, like a crazed dog after its own tail, picturing exactly how *bad* it could be.

'It's just a curtain in a window,' Decker called out.

Haden glanced up and saw, two storeys up, a piece of patterned fabric playing with a breeze.

'But we heard someone.'

'Could've been wrong.'

'Maybe . . .' Haden pushed at the door, which was already slightly ajar, and stepped through the narrow gap into a grand entrance hall. The elegant, arched windows were shuttered and the only light filtered down the wide staircase from the floor above. In the gloom he could see a corridor stretching off to his right, at the end of which an open door beckoned. Ignoring it he crept towards the stairs, dust swirling about his feet.

The broad planks of wood groaned quietly as each step accepted his weight, sounding like they weren't used to the job any more. Haden, finger on the rifle's trigger, staring upwards, made his way slowly to the landing and then on to the first floor. He stood for a minute or so, listening. Nothing. Haden searched the floor he was on, moving quietly from room to room and found nothing, except more evidence that this city had been deserted for quite a long time.

The next floor was where they'd seen the open window but he couldn't hear anyone moving about up there. Should he call out? Or would that be a foolish thing to do – more foolish than being in this house in the first place?

Only one way to find out.

Five minutes later Haden had been through every room on the floor above finding nothing and nobody. He was just about to go to the window and shout to Decker that he'd finished his search and was coming back down when he heard someone call out. The croaky voice of an old man.

'Help me . . . *please* help me!' the voice said. Clear as day.

Haden froze. Where was this man? He'd looked *every*where . . . except the floor above.

Running for the staircase, Haden went up two steps at a time. There *had* been someone here after all! But what was an old man doing all by himself at the top of this huge house? Haden stopped. Maybe he wasn't alone. Maybe it was a trap. Creeping up to the next landing he saw the door at the top of the final flight of stairs was wide open, but access was barred by an ornate metal gate that reminded him of something, but he couldn't think what.

'Help me . . . *please* help me!'

Nearer now, the voice sounded hoarse and there was a rustling noise. And twittering. Haden was positive he could hear twittering. Birds? As he went across the landing and up the stairs he remembered what the gate looked like: the door of a birdcage.

Reaching the wide top step he stopped, unable to make sense of what he was seeing: plants, everywhere . . . light, as if there was no ceiling . . . and he'd been right, there were birds. It was like he was approaching a garden. At the top of a house?

Still not at all sure he wasn't walking into an ambush, Haden kept quiet as he walked over to the doorway and stared through the delicate metal bars, amazed. He *was* looking at a garden. This room, a *huge* space, had a glass roof. It was outside and inside at the same time! Through the fancy latticework he could see a riot of plant life and, on closer inspection, noticed that some of the panes of glass in the roof had cracked and he saw vines and other climbing plants were escaping through the gaps. He tried the gate's handle. It squealed as he turned it, but the gate didn't budge.

'Help me . . . *please* help me!'

Haden stood back and kicked, his boot heel smashing into the handle, and the gate flew open. He ran into the room, ducking low in case he really was a target, scanning left and right as he went, ready to return any fire. But none came and he skidded to a halt, trying to take in where he now found himself, aware that he was standing in long, unkempt grass and that there were *trees* in this place, under each of which was a carpet of at least a couple of seasons of dead leaves. What was this place?

'I'm dying!'

Haden whirled round. 'Where are you? I can't see you!'

'Help me . . . I'm dying!'

'I can't help you if you don't tell me where you are, sir!' At the same time as it dawned on Haden that there was something odd about the way this person was speaking, the same phrases being used over and over again, he saw movement and a flash of colour at the edge of his vision. By the time he'd turned whatever it was had disappeared.

A dying man could not, he reasoned, move that fast.

'Who's there?'

No answer.

A thought occurred to him that it was possible he might be the butt of an annoying joke, but the strange noises from the dense undergrowth kept him alert and ready to shoot at anything that moved. Haden could feel the trickle of sweat running down his back and was aware that he was gritting his teeth as he stared down the barrel of his gun, sweeping his gaze left and right. And then he heard a loud rustling in some dense shrubbery near where he'd just seen the movement. Haden tensed and his finger tightened on the trigger as a large, multi-coloured bird burst into view, its wings stretched out wide.

'*Help me!*' it screeched, flying directly over Haden its long tail nearly touching his head, and landed on a tree behind him.

'A parrot? You're a *parrot*?' Haden could feel his heart beating like a drum. 'I could've . . . I could've *killed* you, you *stupid* bird!'

'*Where* is *everyone?*' the parrot sounded exhausted, at the same time as it vigorously nodded its head up and down. It *looked* remarkably healthy.

'Good question . . .' Haden began to examine his surroundings, taking in the roof's curved glass sides meeting in a tall dome, a space which was almost filled by a cherry tree on the verge of bursting into bloom. He could see there was evidence of a brick pathway running round the outer edges of the space.

'*They've all died* . . .' The parrot's voice faded away and then it coughed pathetically.

Walking along the weed-choked path, Haden discovered a long, caged balcony. The door into it was wide open and he realised that the bird must have been out there and seen their arrival in the square and this had triggered its cries. Carrying on along the path it was clear that the bird had survived because this place, protected by the roof and fed by water from a simple arrangement of gutters, was a small, self-contained world. There was everything here that it needed.

'*Help me!*'

Except, Haden thought as he watched the parrot follow him from tree to bush, companionship. Turning a corner he saw off to one side what appeared to be a room with one of its walls removed. As he got nearer he saw there was an armchair, a small table and a couple of wooden chairs . . . and a bed. A bed with someone lying in it.

'*I'm so tired.*' There was a brittle flutter of wings and the parrot landed on the back of the armchair, looking at Haden with its head on one side. '*So* very *tired . . .*' it whispered.

The figure was curled up, small and almost childlike, under a moth-eaten blanket. All Haden could see, without moving anything, was a mass of iron-grey hair, part of a dry, mummified head and a hand. It was hard to tell, but Haden thought it was probably the body of a man. A very old man who had died up here in this strange garden in the sky all on his own. A sad way to leave the world.

But what did he do now? Go on his way, leaving everything as he'd found it, or set the parrot free? It would obviously be able to survive if left here, but it would be a lonely existence for a creature that so clearly craved company. But outside? What would its chances be like there?

Haden was still trying to make up his mind what he should do when he spotted a brown leather-covered book on the dusty table top. He went over and opened it at random to find its yellowed pages filled with what looked like diary entries, drawings and notation. Turning to the front, he saw the '*THE JOURNAL OF THERASTON MYKRAM*' written on the flyleaf and underlined. At least now he knew who the man was. He flicked through the pages until he found the last entry.

I truly do feel that my own end is finally about to come, he read. *It cannot be long now. I <u>deserve</u> for it not to be <u>too</u> much longer. Waiting to die is a terrible way to spend your days. I think I have been going insane, these last few months (this state of mind would, I am sure, have come on me much sooner, but for Tybal — although now all he does is throw my mad ramblings back at me, which is like looking in the mirror, only to be reminded of how old and ugly you actually are) and now I am tired of living, so <u>very</u> tired. I shall, I think, go and lie down*

There was no full stop and no more writing, so it looked like Theraston Mykram had got his final wish and died soon after his last journal entry leaving behind a small, self-contained world that would go on living without him.

'Well, Tybal,' Haden looked over at the parrot. 'What am I going to do with you?'

'*I think I'm going insane!*'

Haden looked at the parrot for a second or two, then made his mind up. He picked up the journal, went back down the path and out onto the balcony. Putting the book and rifle down he found some bars which had been eaten away by rust and pulled them apart to make a hole big enough for the bird to get out, if it wanted to. Now at least it had a choice.

•

'What happened in there? Who needed help?'

'We were too late. The man who needed help died a long time ago.' Haden held his hand out and, frowning, Decker gave him the reins to his horse. 'I'll tell you everything. But let's go.'

He mounted the horse, slipped his rifle back in its holster and put the book in one of the satchels.

'What's that book?'

'The story of what happened in this place.' Haden looked up at the top building he'd just come from and cupped his hands round his mouth. 'Tybal!'

'Tybal? Decker stopped, one foot in his stirrup. 'Who's that?'

'*Help me!*' came the distant reply, as Decker pulled himself up into his saddle.

Decker glanced at Haden, then followed his gaze and blinked with amazement when he saw a flash of red, blue and green flying into the air.

'A talking *bird*?'

'But what would've happened to Tybal if Haden hadn't let him out, Grampa?'

'I suppose he'd have eventually died a lonely death, just like his owner.'

'Is that why Haden gave him a choice?'

The old man looked out of the window, narrowing his eyes. 'I think it was.'

'It's your story, Grampa,' the boy grinned. 'You must know!'

'True, true . . . and yes, I suppose that is why Haden set the bird free. In a perfect world everyone would have the opportunity to choose how they lived and died. And that's what he gave Tybal.'

'So did the journal Haden took say anything, you know, about what had happened in the city?'

'It did.'

'Aren't you going to tell me?'

'No, not right now.'

'Why not?'

'Because we have some catching up to do. There are a couple of people we can't leave behind.'

'Oh, you mean that boy Mowler and his uncle, Pero Esquabar? What were they really doing in that place up in the mountains?'

'Pulling a tiger's tail.' The old man saw his grandson frowning. 'Playing a very dangerous game . . . shall we join them, where Esquabar has returned from seeing Usshien?'

'Yes!'

11 A PLAN OF ACTION

'USSHIEN WANTS TO SEE something a *week tomorrow*? Did you tell him that wasn't possible?'

'D'you think I'm *completely* mad? Anyway, he didn't wait around for me to answer, just assumed that because he'd said it, it would happen. And don't say "how else would you expect a vicious, evil tyrant to act?" '

'You knew what he was like before we came here.' Mowler watched his uncle pace the basement room they were in. Rubbing his unshaven chin, scratching his tangled hair, sighing loudly and with one eye twitching, he looked like a man who was really and truly at the end of his tether. Which wasn't good . . . not good at all.

'What're we going to do?'

'I had an idea on the way back here and I'm thinking

it over – can't you *see* I'm thinking?' Esquabar stopped next to a workbench that looked like a couple of toolboxes had been turned upside down on it and the contents mixed together.

Mowler watched as he picked up a screwdriver, tapped the palm of his hand with the blade and appeared to drift off into a reverie. This was a habit of his uncle's and it was a bit like watching the fuse on a firework burn down. Was his uncle going to go off in a blaze of ideas, or would all his thinking result in a damp squib?

'Yes! Yes, yes, yes!' Esquabar threw his arms up in the air. 'That's it! What do we *know* works, Mowler?'

'Um, well . . . Phyre? We know *that* works, it's just that it works *too* well.'

'It is a little unstable . . .'

'*Unstable*?' said Mowler. 'We keep blowing things up. Things we don't necessarily *want* to blow up . . . like people. How many soldiers died the other day?'

'Three.'

'We *killed* three more people!'

'We killed three *Sardar* – in certain Territories, you'd get a medal for doing that.' Esquabar tossed the screwdriver over his shoulder; it cartwheeled back onto the workbench and then fell onto the floor. 'A big *gold* medal . . .'

Mowler shrugged. 'If we hadn't spent so much time working on the *other* machine we wouldn't be in such trouble now.'

Esquabar rummaged around in his coat pockets, eventually bringing out a fairly small, but obviously heavier-than-it-looked lump of shiny, honey-coloured metal. 'But *what* a machine, eh, Mowler? Despite it being impossible and against *all* the known Laws of Nature, transmutation works! This *was* a piece of lead, and it is now solid, virtually one hundred percent pure gold.'

'You're not . . .' Mowler's jaw dropped. 'Are you thinking of offering Usshien gold instead of his weapon – is *that* your big idea?'

'I thought we'd agreed I was not a complete madman. Of *course* I'm not going to offer him gold . . . if he ever found out what we could do he'd never let us go. Never.' Esquabar began pacing up and down. 'Look, we have spent a not inconsiderable amount of time and that maniac Usshien's money building *our* Engine and not completing *his* rocket. Which, as he now wants to see it working, is a problem as it's not quite there.

'But as you correctly stated, we *do* know that Phyre works. We also know it's volatile, unpredictable and insanely powerful. But we have got quite a lot of it. Enough, *if* we get it right, to blow Dasmed Usshien and his stinking Sardar to dust.'

'And *if* we get it wrong, Uncle?'

'Positive thoughts, Mowler. From now on, *all* we think are *positive* thoughts . . .'

•

Mowler's eyes were red and watery, as if someone had thrown a handful of fine grit into them. They'd hardly stopped working since his uncle had come back from his last meeting with Usshien four days ago. He felt like he'd been stuck in the living hell of the dark, incredibly hot and fetid basement for ninety-six hours with almost no sleep and precious little food. This was, his uncle said, an unpleasant necessity as Usshien needed to be totally convinced that everything, and more, was being done to meet his deadline – now only four short days away. But, of all the work that they were doing, only some of it had anything to do with completing the rocket.

The rocket. Mowler stood for a moment, staring at the twenty-foot long metal cylinder resting horizontally on three big trestles. With its conical tip and four triangular fins at its base, like the fletches on the end of an arrow, it gave every appearance of being nothing more than a very, very big crossbow bolt.

This was supposed to be Usshien's weapon, which they were *supposed* to be demonstrating *in four days*! Mowler shook his head, a cold shiver running down his back, despite the heat. All they'd done to the rocket was increase the size of its fuel capacity. Which, as there was no way the thing was actually going to fly, wasn't going to help their situation much. But Esquabar had refused to tell him why the changes were being made, saying that he had better things to do than spend any of his valuable time explaining the blindingly obvious.

'Stop gawping – work to do, work to do!' Esquabar appeared from a nearby room like a dog after a rabbit and ran across to a padlocked door. 'That thing's all right for now, we'll get back to it later.'

'What else is there to do to it?' Mowler asked, watching his uncle fumble with a bunch of keys that were attached to his belt by a chain.

'Enough.' Esquabar pulled open the door, an invisible fist of heat pushing him backwards.

Inside the room, which glowed with an intense, iridescent blue, there was what Esquabar called the Transmute Engine. It changed things, turned the common-or-garden into the precious. It would, he promised, change their lives. But not for the better, Mowler knew, if they didn't manage to fool the homicidal maniac who ruled this godforsaken place. *Think positive!* he told himself as he followed his uncle through the doorway. *Think positive!*

'Right!' Esquabar pulled up a pair of goggles hanging round his neck and rubbed his hands together. 'Let's make our fortune!'

12 A STOP ALONG THE WAY

THE WALLS OF THE DEAD city of Jardesh were by now a good few miles distant but the calls for help continued to ring out loud and clear. Tybal, the parrot, had decided to come with Decker and Haden, for now at least. It was the eeriest thing, hearing Theraston Mykram's voice, the voice of an old, very dead man. Sometimes it came from nearby trees, then from way behind, then swooping out of the sky, but always declaring the man's insanity and his ultimate loneliness.

At first Decker found this so upsetting he began insisting that they put the bird out of its misery by shooting it, until Haden finally managed to persuade him that the parrot really was fine and that if they called out some new things, maybe it would learn to say them instead. Unfortunately, like an old dog, Tybal didn't appear to be up to much when it came to learning new tricks and by the time dusk began to fall he still hadn't changed his tune.

'Where are we now?'

'Not sure, Deck . . .' Haden reached into first one of the saddlebags and then the other before he found what he wanted. 'Better look at the map, eh?'

'What could've happened back there?'

'In Jardesh?'

Decker nodded.

'Dunno . . . have to read that old man's book to find out. Don't know that I want to, though.'

'*Save me.*' Tybal whispered as he flew past.

'It was something bad and probably best left buried . . .' Haden spread the map out in front of him, angled so the last of the sun's light fell on it. 'Another day's ride and we *should* be near the these foothills, see?' Haden pointed. 'Rafus has marked a small town there, a place called Chamat and I remember something in his journal about it. I think there's an inn, or at least a place where we can stay.'

'A roof, some food and a bed,' Decker smiled. 'That'd be good.'

Haden folded the map up and put it away. 'Let's hope it is. Once we leave Chamat all we have to look forward to is Ghadra and dealing with the Sardar in their home territory.'

'We still going to do this thing?'

'*I* have to, Deck. You don't. Got to do it for my dad –
he'd have gone, if he'd've been asked, so I don't have
much choice. *And* there's nothing else I have to do. But,
like I say, you don't have to come with me . . .'

'*I think I'm going insane!*'

Decker whirled round in his saddle, making a grab
for his pistol.

'Gonna shut that bird up for good if it . . . !'

'It's OK, Deck! We'll stop now, make camp and have
some food. It'll soon be dark and he'll go to sleep.'

'It's like a ghost, Haden, a ghost following us
wherever we go . . . I don't like it.'

'I know you don't.'

'But I'm coming with you, whatever. Bird or no bird.
You've stuck by me, and I'll stick by you. That's the
way it has to be, otherwise there'll be nothing left. No
one to remember with.'

They awoke to a cold, damp dawn, Haden still with
Theraston Mykram's book clutched to his chest. His
head was full of the things the old man had written as
they set about re-lighting the fire. After a quick meal,
sharing the last of their bread with Tybal, who politely
said 'thank you' every time he was given food, Haden
and Decker moved off. It was a good day's ride to
Chamat and both of them were eager to get to some
kind of friendly civilisation, even though every mile
they rode brought them a mile nearer to the Sardar.

Whatever they'd come up against so far on their journey, Haden knew it was more than likely that the dangers they'd face in Ghadra would be far greater. And they'd be walking into them with their eyes wide open. Idiots going where the bravest men might well choose not to.

These thoughts harried and pestered him as he rode; he believed he was doing the right thing; he believed Decker was coming with him willingly and that he didn't hold any responsibility for that, except it felt like he should. He had brought Decker along with him, after all. But then again, he couldn't have left him behind. Whatever happened, he supposed, their lives – short or long – were going to be far more exciting (and, if they succeeded, more useful) than if they'd simply been played out in Starpoint.

Ahead lay mystery – what was going on in Ghadra?

Ahead lay problems – how were they ever going to meet up with Rafus's associate, Blade?

And ahead lay unknown perils, maybe their own deaths . . .

Haden knew he had to carry on, to see where the path he'd been pointed towards took him, but he didn't want to die. He'd hardly lived! There was so much else to do!

'We'll be all right.'

Decker's words broke Haden's train of thought.

'What?'

'Stop worrying – you've been twisting those reins and frowning the last half mile or so.'

'Just thinking . . .' Haden shivered involuntarily. 'My mother used to say that an angel was walking across my grave when that happened.'

'They don't know everything, mothers.' Decker smiled. 'We'll be fine. Just have to stick together.'

Haden regarded his friend, this person he'd grown up believing a dull fool but who had turned out to be quite the opposite, and he shook his head. 'Sorry, Deck.'

'For what?'

'For – I don't know – everything . . .'

'Don't look back. No point.'

The rest of the day was just a slog, no time for anything but putting as many miles behind them as they could; they ate in the saddle, hardly talked and pushed their horses hard. Tybal stayed with them, in the end deciding that flying was too much of an effort and it would be easier if he hitched a ride; he chose Haden's shoulder as his perch.

The sun was setting, a chill breeze blowing up, when they eventually crested a hill and saw their destination. In the valley below them, spread out on a dark green tablecloth, was the small town of Chamat. Thin plumes of blue-grey smoke trickled upwards from almost every chimney and they could see people moving about without using Rafus's binoculars. The place was probably twice the size of Starpoint, before the Sardar had reduced it to ashes and memories, but it was still small, a village not unlike the one they had known so well. The sight of it made the two friends pull their horses up and look at each other.

'Strange . . .' Haden swallowed hard.

'Like home, but . . . but different.'

Haden geed his horse. 'Come on.'

'Wait!'

'Eh?' Haden turned in his saddle, Tybal squawking as he almost lost his balance. 'What's the matter?'

'We should be careful. Remember what people thought about strangers, back in Starpoint.'

Jerking on his reins, Haden guided his horse back up the slope. 'How'd you mean?'

'They won't trust us, will they? They'll want to know where we're from, who we are, where we're going. All those kind of questions. What're we going to tell 'em?'

'Little as possible?'

Decker shook his head 'Unanswered questions make people suspicious.'

'True. I always got in far less trouble when my lies were as close to the truth as I could get them.' Haden shrugged. 'How about we just say we're from the Outlands, that we're looking for work anywhere we can get it? Don't volunteer any information, play it by ear, like my dad used to say.'

'My dad . . .' Decker looked away. 'He just used to clip *my* ear.'

'He'd have a shock if he could see you now.'

'Yeah . . . the things I'd to say to him.'

•

The ghostly wisps of a thin mist had risen up by the time they found themselves approaching the twilit village. The dull, soft glow of oil lamps flickered in most of the windows of the one- and two-storey houses up ahead, and on the air they caught the smell of meals being cooked. It made their mouths water and their stomachs growl in anticipation.

Something about being near a place with streets and houses made Tybal jittery. He stayed put on Haden's shoulder but he bobbed up and down nervously muttering '*Oh dear*' and '*Save me*' and '*Help*' to himself.

'It's all right boy, it's all right . . .' Haden reached up and stroked the parrot's head. Ahead, where the rough track they were on met the first houses, he could see a small knot of men. He could see they'd been spotted, but there was something about the way these people were acting. If they were a 'welcoming committee', then they weren't looking so friendly.

'We don't look like Sardar, do we, Deck?'

'Hope not.'

Haden casually pulled his jacket back so he could get to his pistol easier; the last thing he was looking for was a fight, but best to be prepared. They rode on, the steady beat of their horses' hooves like a lazy drum roll announcing their arrival. A few yards from where the men were standing, gathered round an unlit brazier, the travellers stopped.

'Is this Chamat?' Haden asked as casually as he could.

The men looked up at him, their eyes suspiciously flicking across to Decker and back again. Haden couldn't see any weapons but knew that meant nothing.

'That a parrot?' one of them asked.

'*I'm going insane!*' said Tybal before Haden could reply. '*Help me!*'

There was a long moment of silence during which Tybal stretched his red, blue and yellow wings wide, folded them carefully back and nuzzled at Haden's ear. Then one of the men laughed and the tension broke like a soap bubble bursting.

'Where'd you get him?'

'J—'

'Just found him,' Decker butted in. 'Or should say he found us, couple of days back.'

'Where've you come from?'

Haden looked at Decker, who he knew had stopped him from mentioning the name Jardesh in case these people knew something about what had happened there that they didn't.

'The Outlands,' he replied.

'Big place,' said one man, Haden didn't see which.

'Not if you've got ambition it isn't.' Haden watched the men now roughly spread across the road and barring the way into the village, and tried to work out which one was the leader. He'd be the one they'd have to convince.

'What d'you want here?' said a man standing at the back of the group. The rest turned to look at him.

'A meal, a drink, stabling for the horses . . .'

'. . . and a bed for me,' added Decker. 'I want a proper bed for the night. A soft one.'

'Sore arse, eh?' commented one of the men near the front, the one who'd laughed at Tybal. Decker grinned sheepishly and nodded.

'Can you direct us where to go?' Haden allowed his horse to move forward a couple of steps.

'Maybe.' The man at the back walked to the front and Haden could see he had a rifle held in the crook of his arm. 'You two seen anyone on your ride here?'

'A few people . . . we've mostly tried to keep ourselves to ourselves.' Haden looked pointedly at the man with the rifle. 'Less trouble that way.'

'Where're you headed?'

'We heard there was work in Quadrine, maybe Cherinna . . . going to look there.'

'Well, take my advice and steer well clear of the Thunder Road.'

'Never heard of the place – Deck?' Haden glanced at Decker, who shook his head.

'So you'll be leaving tomorrow, then?'

'Wouldn't want to outstay our welcome, sir.'

The man stood back and motioned with his rifle barrel. 'Make sure you don't . . .'

•

The inn wasn't hard to find. Like the bars back home had been, it appeared to be at the centre of the village's life, with lights blazing from every window in its two storeys and a good number of horses tethered outside. After sorting out the stabling and being made to pay in full in advance, the two friends took their bags and traipsed back round to the entrance.

'Suspicious lot in this place,' Decker grunted as they went up the steps to the raised veranda that ran the length of the inn. 'What's the Thunder Road?'

'No idea, but back there didn't seem like the time and place to ask.'

'Reckon not . . .'

The smell of cooking, smoke and beer hit them as they walked into the large, low-ceilinged room. They both stopped, took a deep breath and exhaled slowly as they took in where they were.

Various rough wooden tables and benches, most of them occupied, filled the floorspace and over to the right a bar ran the whole way down one side of the room. Behind it three men and a young boy served customers and filled orders from a couple of waitresses.

'I am thirsty.' Haden let the door swing closed behind him as he set off towards one of the few empty tables he could see.

The sight of Tybal balanced on Haden's shoulder drew a fair amount of curious attention but not enough to make them feel at all worried.

'Beer?' Haden asked, putting his saddlebags and holstered rifle down.

'Two.' Decker stuck up both thumbs and grinned.

'You eating as well?'

They both looked round at the waitress who'd materialised by their table.

'Whatever you've got – we haven't had a proper meal in days.' Haden watched the waitress weigh them up and he made no bones about doing the same to her: not young, not old, a strong, almost-quite-pretty, don't-mess-with-me face. 'You got rooms for rent?'

'*A* room. You'll have to share. And pay . . .'

' . . . in advance.' Haden nodded. 'We know the rules, already stabled our horses.'

The waitress held out a hand, rubbing her thumb against her forefinger. 'Only metal, we don't take any of that paper money.'

'We don't carry it.' Haden showed the woman a selection of silver and bronze coins from at least three different Territories. This would not be the kind of place to let it be known you had any gold currency.

'How much?'

The woman raised one eyebrow and made a thoughtful face; Haden knew she was calculating exactly how much she could get away with overcharging these two visitors. And he also reckoned that by weight alone, forget face value, one of the larger silver coins, or two of the smaller ones, would be more than enough to cover everything they wanted.

'I see you've travelled,' the woman reached out and picked up one large and one small silver coin.

'*A* room for a night, and two meals.' Haden looked quizzically at the woman. 'You charging for the parrot?'

'I, ah, I must've misheard . . .'

The small silver coin dropped back onto Haden's palm.

'Noisy in here, ma'am.'

'That it is.'

'*That it certainly is.*'

'Clever,' the waitress glanced at Tybal, 'for a bird.'

13   A Branch Snaps

Haden fell asleep wondering what had prompted Tybal, out of the blue, to copy – *almost* copy – what the waitress had said. Maybe it was a phrase the old man, Theraston Mykram, had used. When he woke up, it seemed like only minutes later, he found the morning sun streaming through the threadbare curtains of the room's one small window.

Decker was still gently snoring on the lumpy palliasse next to him and Tybal was perched, eyes shut, feathers fluffed up, on the back of a rickety old chair. Getting up, Haden checked out of the window and reckoned it was at least a couple of hours since sunrise; time to be making a move. He didn't want to give anyone the chance to try and charge them for another day's stay.

'Time to greet the day, Deck!' said Haden, nudging Decker's shoulder with his foot.

'*Greet the day, come out and play, my lovely boy!*'

Tybal obviously knew the childhood rhyme his mother had never stopped using. Haden looked over at the parrot, stretching his wings and nonchalantly starting to preen his feathers. A stab of pain gripped his stomach, the sharpness of his loss cutting like a razor: his mother, his whole family and life were *gone*! These last few days there had been so many other things to think about and deal with that the rawness of their deaths had been numbed. Now it was back, bringing with it a visceral need for revenge, rising like bile and leaving a bitter, acid taste in his mouth.

Haden looked down at Decker, still sleeping soundly, picked his boots up and left the room.

They had eaten breakfast mostly in silence. Only when they were re-saddling the horses did Haden finally explain about Tybal repeating his mother's rhyme; how it had brought everything back and put him in such a foul mood. He started to apologise but Decker stopped him, folding him in a bear hug and sobbing like a lost child, a sight that had scared off the stable lads.

Neither of them looked back as they left Chamat. It wasn't a place they were likely to come back to, or ever regret leaving. They had been vague about their intentions, hinting that the plan was to make for

Quadrine, that particular territory being in the opposite direction to Ghadra. Only once they were a couple of pine-forested valleys away from Chamat did they start to look for a route that would take them back on the right track.

Because of the detour they found themselves having to make their own path through the densely packed pine trees, relying completely on Rafus's compass to keep them from wandering in circles. It was not the easiest of journeys and it was slow, with the two friends having to concentrate as the horses carefully picked their way. As if aware that he too might get lost Tybal stayed put on Haden's shoulder, looking and listening.

The forest was alive with the scurryings and whispers, squawks and tappings of a thousand invisible creatures nesting, eating, hunting and dying; sounds, like the painted backdrop in a chapel play, that went completely unnoticed after a while. And then, for some reason, there was a lull, as if a band leader had swept his baton flat and ordered instantaneous silence from the forest orchestra.

In this unexpected quiet the sound of dry wood cracking rang out like a distant pistol shot.

'We're being followed.' Decker slowly turned in his saddle, the leather creaking.

Haden slipped to the ground. He got Tybal to climb onto his hand, then gave him and his reins to Decker.

'Tie the horses up, take the rifle and get out of sight,' he whispered. The parrot cocked his head to one side and looked down at him. 'You stay, and you be quiet, Tybal.'

'This a good idea, Haden?'

'Got to find out who it is.'

'And?'

Haden shrugged. He didn't know what he was going to do, except that if it was a Sardar, he'd kill him. Unsheathing his dagger, he moved away. In his head he could hear his father's voice, giving instructions to him and his younger brother on the tricks and ruses you could use to move as silent as a breeze, and he followed them to the letter.

Circling back the way they'd come, he padded like a village cat stalking an unwary mouse . . . move, stop, listen, look, wait, listen, then move again . . . his breathing shallow, his heartbeat slow and steady. He was surprised how calm and controlled he felt, how good it was to concentrate every sense on one task. The blood sang in his ears as he looked harder than he ever had, listened as if his life depended on it (which it well might) and kept himself ready to make his move the moment he needed to.

Haden had no idea how long it was before he saw shadows move in a way they shouldn't and it took his eyes a moment to translate the signs as a man leading a horse. There the man was, some twenty feet away, creeping as quietly as he could along the track Haden and Deck had made. Haden was startled to realise that he recognised him: it was the man with the rifle and all the questions at the entrance to Chamat last night.

He'd have some questions of his own to answer now!

With this thought uppermost in his mind, Haden started to try and position himself behind the man in order to take him by surprise. But wanting to do something and achieving it are two very different things, as one moment the man was doggedly following his prey, unaware *he* was being followed, and the next he'd swung round. Looking Haden straight in the eye, his lip twisted in a cold smile, the man pointed a hefty pistol at him.

'You're good, boy, but you ain't *that* good. Drop the knife and kiss the dirt.'

If there was one thing that riled Haden more than anything it was being called 'boy'. And when he was angry he didn't think straight; his father had always said he let his temper get the better of him.

'I said drop the knife, boy,' the man growled. There was a loud click as he pulled the pistol's hammer back. 'You see I mean business, right?'

Haden knew that the sensible thing was to do as he'd been told, but there was a heat in his veins that overpowered wisdom and logic. So instead he did the unexpected: he flung himself sideways, at the same time throwing his arm forward with all the force he could muster, the sudden movement spooking the man's horse. With a high-pitched whinny it reared and cantered off.

Haden had surprise on his side, and he was fast. The blade of his perfectly balanced dagger sliced through the man's right bicep just as he pulled the trigger, and the bullet that was meant to tear a hole in Haden's chest merely grazed his rib cage. As Haden hit the ground, so did the man's pistol. Now the gloves were off! Quick as a whip Haden was up, but instead of going for the pistol, his anger focussed on the man and he went for him.

'You . . .' with an agonised roar the man swatted Haden out of the way as he tore the dagger out of his arm and knocked the younger man down, winding him, ' . . . are gonna pay for this, boy!'

Gulping air like a fish out of water, Haden stumbled to his feet as the man, blood streaming down his arm and dripping off his fingers, scooped up the pistol with his left hand.

'Hope you're ready to meet your maker, boy . . .'

'*I'm going insaaaaane!*'

A screeching flash of red, blue and green appeared out of nowhere, flew between Haden and the man, and was gone. Haden was taken by surprise by Tybal's sudden appearance, but the man from Chamat looked like he'd been struck by lightning, shocked rigid by the sight. Then, before either of them could react, a voice rang out.

'Drop the gun!'

Decker's voice sounded as if he was quite near, somewhere behind the now wide-eyed man. And then gunfire, a bullet chewing a bite out of a tree inches from the man's face, spitting tiny, hot splinters at him and making him flinch. Haden heard the unmistakable *K-CHUNKK* sound of a bolt-action rifle being reloaded.

'Now I'm aiming at your ear.'

Decker move out into the open. The man's shoulders slumped when he saw him and he dropped the pistol on the ground.

'And the dagger,' said Haden, only now aware of the hot, stinging pain in his side where the bullet had kissed him and left. There was a flutter of wings and Tybal swooped down onto his shoulder. 'Now kick them both away.'

'Who is he?' Decker pushed his way through a tangle of undergrowth.

'He was the one asking the questions last night . . .' Haden, keeping a wary eye on the man, bent down and picked up the pistol and his dagger, which he wiped on his trousers.

'Why'd he follow us?'

Haden stared at the man, his eyebrows raised questioningly. 'Well, you heard him. Why?'

The man, who was gripping his arm in a vain attempt to stem the flow of blood steadily trickling off his fingers, scowled and looked away.

'*Why, oh why, oh why?*'

The man glanced at Tybal, his face now pale and strained, but still said nothing. Without warning Decker slammed the rifle butt against his injured arm.

'Don't like being followed,' said Decker, watching the man stagger, then hold onto a tree to stop himself from falling over.

'Go . . . to Hell . . .' The man grimaced, his breath coming in short and shallow gasps, blood drip, drip, dripping onto the pine needles.

'You'll get there a long time before either of us, the rate you're going.' Haden glanced down at the ragged hole and small bloodstain on his own shirt. 'Answer the question and I'll put a tourniquet on your arm, bandage it up. You won't last long if I don't.'

The man slid slowly to the ground. 'I get paid . . .' he grunted. 'Paid to keep my eyes open, report what I see.'

'Who to?' Haden signalled to Decker that he should get something for the man's arm. 'Who's interested in us?'

'It's not you, in particular . . . could be anyone,' the man looked to see if Decker was coming back. 'You two, your story didn't fit. Outland boys with fancy saddles, nice rifle, good horses? And with the kind of money Tarny said you had . . .'

'Tarny?'

'Woman at the inn.'

Haden nodded to himself. 'Who pays you, then?'

'The people where you're headed to.'

'And where d'you think that is?'

'The Thunder Road.'

'Told you last night, we don't know where that is.'

'Then why make the big detour so's it don't look like you're going there?'

Haden frowned. 'You're working for the Sa . . .' he stopped himself, realising that he'd just confirmed the man's suspicions.

'I work for whoever pays, and right now it's the people up in Ghadra.'

Conflicting emotions battled for dominance in Haden's confused head. Part of him screamed that he should beat this man to a pulp for his venal association with the Sardar, for taking their blood money, while a more considered voice said there was information – *valuable information!* – to be gained from him. The quiet, steady voice eventually won the day and he unclenched his fists.

'So what is this "Thunder Road"?' Haden asked, watching Decker kneel down and tie a piece of cord round the man's upper arm.

'Round here, that's the name for the way into Ghadra, least that's what it's been called since the explosions up there . . .' the man winced as Decker tightened the cord.

'Explosions?'

'They got themselves some kind of sciencer . . .'

'Esquabar, Pero Esquabar.' Haden nodded to himself.

'You know a lot, for an Outland boy.'

'I'm no one's "boy", least of all yours – what's this Esquabar been doing?'

'No idea, but Usshien gets the man whatever he wants, and he wants a *lot* of raw materials.'

Haden pushed himself off the tree he'd been leaning against. 'Finish the bandage and let's go, Deck.'

'What you gonna do with me?'

'Take your horse and leave you to find your own way home,' Haden said, walking off.

Behind him there was a sound like a green branch snapping. Haden looked round to see Decker standing up; the man appeared to have fallen asleep, his head lolling forward.

'Didn't have any choice,' Decker shrugged. 'Knew too much about us.'

'*Save me . . .*' Tybal bowed up and down on Haden's shoulder. '*Save me!*'

'Too late for that, bird.' Decker stood up and wiped his hands on his trousers. 'Much too late . . .'

*• ✳ • *

The old man looked over at his grandson. 'Are you all right, Mykel? You look sad.'

'I didn't want Decker to do that, Grampa . . .'

'He didn't want to do it. He had to.' The old man got up and went over to sit next to his grandson, putting an arm around him. 'Truth is, sometimes good people have to do bad things to survive and if I told you this story any other way I'd just be making it up. This is how everything happened, but if you don't like it I'll stop.'

'No, Grampa! Don't stop, I want the real story! It's just because it was Decker . . .'

'You mean you wouldn't have been surprised if Haden had done it?'

Mykel shook his head. 'I suppose not . . . I mean how did he know what to do?'

'Decker? He'd wrung enough chickens' necks in his time, he knew how to make it quick and quiet.'

Mykel nodded to himself then looked up at his grandfather. 'So were they a long way from Ghadra, did they have far to go?'

'They surely did. It was quite a journey, and events were moving on as they were making it . . .'

14 THE ENGINE ROOMS

THE TRANSMUTE ENGINE WASN'T really an *engine* in that it wasn't in any way a machine that converted power into motion, like the Phyre-fuelled one they'd built and installed in the rocket. It wasn't really a machine at all. It was like some huge glass and steel beast, a sharp-angled, hot, dangerous animal that snaked through two of the basement rooms, hissing, gurgling and demanding to be fed, watered and looked after or it would blow up.

The heat, the noise and the smells in the Engine rooms were like a physical assault, in themselves more than enough to keep anyone unwanted from trying to find out what Mowler and his uncle were up to. The recent lethal accident had pretty much guaranteed them the privacy they needed – no one in their right mind would come down here now.

He, therefore, must be completely *out* of his mind, Mowler thought to himself as he emptied a carboy of acid into an open sluice. Why did his whole life revolve around highly volatile substances which might explode at any moment? If his mother had known what her brother was going to get up to then he was positive she'd *never* have let her only son go off with him.

His uncle came into the room as Mowler was hammering a cork bung into the neck of the empty carboy.

'We're running out of acid,' Mowler said, peering through the thick glass of his leather goggles; sweat was pouring off him and he could barely see a thing.

'Take a break, I'll join you in a minute,' Pero Esquabar inspected a couple of valves and tapped a pressure gauge with his knuckle. 'And stay inside, I don't want anyone reporting back to Usshien that we were slacking.'

Mowler left the room at a trot, shutting the door behind him. His eyes felt red raw, like his throat, and he needed liquid and *lots* of it. Peeling off his thick steel-reinforced leather gloves, he removed his goggles, heavy apron, filthy once-white coat and the sweat-soaked neckerchief from around his head and immediately felt quite light-headed. He was exhausted. They'd worked all night and he knew there was precious little chance that there'd be any time for a proper rest today. They were on a gruelling schedule.

He dragged himself up the stairs and stopped as he went into the room that served as their kitchen. The atmosphere . . . it smelled, what was the word? Ah, yes – *fresh*! Mowler took a deep breath and started hacking, his lungs protesting at this invasion of untainted air. The coughing fit dislodged some phlegm in his throat and he spat out something thick and green – if he didn't get blown to smithereens first, it seemed more and more likely that he'd probably die from being poisoned.

Hauling open the door of the large clay brick 'cool chest' (another of his uncle's inventions) he grabbed a jug of water and drank from it. The cold liquid spilled down his chin and felt like an ice blade in his throat. Mowler wished there was enough of it to dive into.

The combination of tiredness and hunger made it hard to think straight but there was a lot to think about. If everything went according to his uncle's plan, then in less than two days he was going to be an extremely rich nephew; if, on the other hand, something went even just a tiny bit wrong (and he'd been with Uncle Pero long enough to know that if something could go wrong it often did), they would both be very *dead*.

As he saw things the chances of success were so small you'd need a magnifying glass to see them. In his opinion it was a toss-up between that lunatic Dasmed Usshien discovering they weren't doing what he was paying them to do, and something blowing up. Mowler's shoulders slumped as the reality of his own imminent demise hit him.

'Think positive, Mowler!'

Pero Esquabar patted his nephew on the shoulder as he strode past him, gloves in hand, goggles pushed up on his head and still wearing his apron, and picked an apple that had seen far better days off the table.

'But, uncle . . .'

'No "buts",' Esquabar took a bite out of the fruit and chewed. 'We must concentrate *all* our energies on the rocket.'

'What about the Engine?'

'I've just shut it down.'

Mowler looked puzzled.

'We've made all the gold and diamonds we can reasonably take with us, no point in carrying on,' Esquabar stopped chewing, glanced quizzically at what he was eating, frowned and threw what was left of the apple away. 'We can always make more later.'

'D'you *really* think we can get away with it – what if Usshien finds out?' This was Mowler's least favourite outcome as he was sure it would mean a long, slow, painful death. If you were going to *have* to die, he reasoned, quickly was the better option.

'He won't, nephew, he won't. Have faith, this *will* work!'

Mowler sighed and shrugged.

'You're just tired. Have a sleep,' Esquabar patted Mowler on the shoulder again as he strode back out of the room. 'There are some calculations I have to go over before we can carry on . . . I'll come and get you.'

Mowler watched his uncle go. Sleep. Or eat? He shook his head, he could always sleep later, because, if the Fates weren't with them, this might well be the last meal he ever ate . . .

15   Paths Cross

THE RAIN FELL LIKE it was being poured from a bucket somewhere high up above, drops the size of small pebbles pounding them incessantly and the noise was a dull, flat, continuous roar. It had been raining solidly, with no let-up, since the night before and, from what Haden could see of the lead-grey sky through the trees, it wasn't going to stop any time soon. Apart from being soaked to the bone he was cold, tired, hungry and his side ached where the bullet had not-quite missed him.

They had been climbing steadily since early morning and the pines were beginning to thin out. He was in the lead with the compass and a disconsolate, bedraggled Tybal hunched on his shoulder, and Decker behind, leading the dead man's horse.

The dead man . . .

They hadn't said a word about what had happened since leaving the body slumped against a tree for the carrion-eaters to deal with. Even when Decker had been helping Haden clean and bandage the red-raw furrow in his side the matter had been left undiscussed; he didn't know quite what to say, and Decker certainly didn't seem to want to talk about it. The rest of the day had been spent trying to make the best time they could in the general direction of Ghadra, stopping the previous evening at dusk and making camp just before the weather turned.

Haden knew that, in the heat of combat, he'd wanted to kill the Sardar spy and would've had no qualms about doing so. What he struggled to come to terms with was how simple it had been for Decker to decide what to do, in cold blood. And then do it. There was no doubt it had been the logical move to make for someone who was used to killing people . . . executing them. But that wasn't the way they'd grown up at Starpoint, and what Decker had done now cast him in an entirely different light. Haden looked over his shoulder.

'Want to stop?' he called out.

'Want this *rain* to stop.' Decker yelled back.

'*Stop! Stop! Stop!*'

'Some hope . . .' Haden knew exactly how the bird felt.

'Much further to Ghadra?'

'No idea,' Haden shook his head and pulled his

sodden hood further forward in a vain attempt to keep the rain off his face. His world was now the narrow oval window in front of him, his view just various shades of grey, vertical lines; wherever he turned, all he could see was the cold monochrome of the trees and the rain-filled spaces between them. Right now he could not imagine what it would be like to be dry and warm . . . had he *ever* been dry and warm?

Ten, maybe fifteen minutes later (he'd no idea of the passage of time, and had lost track of how long they'd been travelling as well), Haden saw something move, or thought he did. Turning to try and catch sight of it again, there was nothing.

'Did you see that, Deck?' Haden reined in his horse.

'What?'

'Something up ahead . . . I'm sure I saw something.'

Decker's pulled his horse up next to Haden and looked over at him, grinning. 'Must've been a fish.'

'Could've been a duck.' Haden smiled back.

'Or – or a person,' Decker's eyes widened, 'you could've seen a person . . .'

Haden frowned at Decker, whose expression had just changed from amused to perplexed. 'Out here?'

Decker gave a hurried nod. 'Yeah, a person with a, um . . . with a gun in my back.'

'Don't try *any*thing.' The voice was a husky whisper, only just audible above the rain. 'You got a pistol, you give it to me slowly,' the voice said, 'and make sure it's grip first.'

Decker obliged, pulling the dead man's repeater out of his belt and handing it behind him by the barrel. Then Haden saw a stick, a gun-shaped piece of branch, land a few feet in front of him . . .

'*Help me!*'

'Who's that?' The voice sounded surprised.

For a second Haden wondered if he could use this revelation of a 'third' person to his advantage, but realised the odds were stacked against him. He'd make far too much noise trying to get to his own pistol, which was trapped under the saturated folds of dark green oilcloth he was wrapped in.

'It's a parrot.' Haden had counted to four, waiting to see what would happen, before he heard the sound of the repeater's hammer being cocked.

'Where's Rafus?'

Haden and Decker frowned at each other.

'I said "where's Rafus?". It's a simple question, now answer it.'

A boy-like, ragged figure, crouching as it came into Haden's view, pointed the pistol rock steady with two mud-streaked hands. Haden stared, nonplussed. It was a woman! Her hair was cut short, face scratched, her clothes filthy and torn. But it was still a woman. And someone – out here in the unending grey of this drowned wilderness – who knew Rafus! Haden's brain, confused for more than a moment, finally put all the pieces together in the right order.

'Sergeant Blade?' he queried.

'Blade?' echoed Decker.

'How'd you know my name?' The woman's eyes narrowed suspiciously. 'And – *where* – is – Rafus?'

She punctuated her angry words by jabbing the pistol, and through the blur of rain it seemed to Haden that her trigger finger was straining to do its job.

'He's dead,' said Decker. 'The Sardar killed him. We buried him.'

'Help me . . . I'm dying!'

No one spoke, no one moved for a long time after that and an observer, had one chanced upon the scene, might have thought they were looking at an eerie tableau.

'How do I know you're not lying through your dratted teeth?'

Haden couldn't be sure but he thought he saw the trigger finger relax, slightly.

'You don't,' he said, hoping for the best. 'But trust me, we're telling the truth . . .'

The rain had finally slowed to a drizzle and, underneath cover provided by the tarps they'd strung between a couple of trees, the three of them huddled round a fire that was more smoke than heat. Tybal, fluffed up and perched on a branch, watched in stony silence. They weren't by any means dry, but at least they weren't getting any wetter and the uneasy truce seemed to be holding.

'Rafus gave us everything before he died.' Haden nodded at the saddlebags next to him and jerked a thumb at the horses tethered nearby. 'We didn't steal anything.'

'What were you two doing out in the Plains anyway?' Sgt Blade sat cross-legged opposite him, the repeater cradled easily in her lap.

'Tracking the Sardar who'd destroyed Starpoint,' Haden watched Decker feed some damp twigs to the fire. 'Where we come . . . *came* from.'

'That was the place Rafus was making for.'

Haden nodded. 'He was looking for my father.'

'*You're* Akatine's son?'

'You knew him too?'

'Knew *of* him,' Sgt Blade carefully studied Haden as she talked. 'Before my time, but they still tell the stories.'

'What's *your* story?'

Haden and Sgt Blade turned to look at Decker, still tending the fire.

'Mine?' she said.

'Looks like you got one to tell.' Decker leant forward and blew gently on the small pyramid of twigs and needles, its tiny heart glowing redder with every breath.

'While Rafus went to find Akatine,' Sgt Blade glanced at Haden, 'I followed the trail of men and materials that led to Ghadra. My job was to get myself into the city and try to find out what they were doing.'

'How'd you do?' Haden opened one of the saddlebags and took out a couple of cloth bundles.

Blade looked down at herself and grimaced. 'Not so good. My plan was to infiltrate one of the caravans taking supplies to Ghadra but I got careless at the smelting works. Someone found me poking my nose in where it wasn't wanted.'

'How'd you get away?' Haden unwrapped one of the bundles to reveal the loaf of bread and large piece of cheese that they'd bought before leaving Chamat the previous morning.

'They were even more careless: they didn't find my knife.'

'How many'd you kill?' Decker asked.

'Two.' Blade reached into her grubby tunic and came out with a thin, slightly curved dagger in her hand; she started cutting the bread, then looked at Haden and Decker, one eyebrow raised. 'I cleaned it.'

'What were you doing out here?' Haden unwrapped the second package, a large hunk of pale grey salted meat.

'Getting away. I escaped a few days ago . . . was trying to find the route Rafus might take to get to Ghadra. See if I could meet up with him.'

'The Sardar following you?' Decker waved a cloud of smoke out of his face.

'I doubt it. One Quadrine spy wouldn't be worth the effort.'

'They knew you were a spy, not a thief?' Haden asked, cutting some strips off the meat with his own knife.

'Like I said, I was careless.'

'What you gonna do now?' Decker asked.

'Rest up a bit, I'm tired.'

'So very, very tired . . .'

'Where'd you get that damn bird?'

'Found him in Jardesh,' Haden said, and heard Decker's sharp intake of breath.

'You went there, to the plague city?' Sgt Blade sat back and picked up the gun she'd taken off Decker and cocked it. 'How long ago?'

'There was no one there, the place was deserted . . .'

'They all died, that's why. How long ago were you there?'

'Three days,' said Decker, firmly. 'Three days ago, and nothing wrong with us.'

'No rashes?'

'Nothing.' Decker fed more twigs to the fire.

'We're fine,' Haden gestured at Decker and himself. 'Really.'

'How can you be sure?' Blade still looked very skeptical about the situation. 'How'd you *know*?'

'They didn't *all* die. I found a book, a journal,' Haden said. 'The old man who wrote it survived for a long time and he listed the symptoms and what happened to people who caught the illness. We've had nothing.'

'Why . . .'

'We didn't know anything about the place,' Haden interrupted Blade's question. 'I saw the name on a map, and I wanted to find out what a city was like.'

Blade relaxed slightly. 'Is that why you're going to Ghadra, too?'

Haden shook his head. 'Started out just wanting revenge, find some Sardar and kill them for what they did to my family. I did that . . . well, I managed to kill one of them at least. That was when we found Rafus – and found out why he was looking for my father.

'Just before Rafus died he asked me to finish the job he'd started. My father would've gone with him, I know he would . . .' Haden fell silent for a moment, then took a deep breath. 'So I'm going to Ghadra for the same reasons you are.'

'What about you?' Blade asked Decker.

'Where he goes, I go.'

Blade uncocked the pistol and Haden could see the tension seep out of her body; her calculating, green eyes flicked left and right as she surveyed the makeshift campsite.

'You two,' she said finally, 'you want to come with me?'

'Maybe you want to come with *us*?' Decker reached over and took a piece of salted meat. 'We're the ones with the extra horse.'

'And maps, a compass, money, food . . .' Rafus's pistol was now in Haden's hand. 'And guns.'

'You think you can do this without me?'

'I think we got this far *without* your help, sergeant,' Haden said, sounding a lot more confident than he actually felt.

'You really are a chip off the old block.'

'What d'you mean?'

'Rafus always said your father was brave "to the point of pig-headed stubbornness",' Blade made quote marks with her fingers. 'Looks like you take after him.'

Haden glanced at Decker, then away and swallowed hard. All this talk of his father and how like him he appeared to be brought back a lot of harrowing, unwanted memories. All he hoped was that, however all this worked out, he'd make his father proud . . .

•✶•

'Why's Sgt Blade so suspicious, Grampa?'

'She may not have been in uniform, but she was still army, Mykel, and soldiers never trust civilians, always think they act like sheep. Strange, when you consider it's the soldiers who're trained not to think for themselves and follow orders, no matter what.'

The boy thought about what he'd been told for a moment or two. 'But wasn't it a bit of a coincidence?'

'What?' The old man looked over at his grandson.

'Them all meeting up like that.'

'Luck.'

'Sorry?'

'It was luck, chance, fate, call it what you will, but happy – and unhappy – accidents happen all the time. You think I'm playing games with the truth?'

'No, Grampa!' The boy looked shocked at the accusation.

'Course not! It's just . . . well, you made the forest sound so big.'

'It was big, but, if paths are meant to cross, in my experience they have a habit of doing so.'

'Did she agree to go with Haden and Decker, then?'

'She didn't really have much choice . . .'

16   A Hornets' Nest

GHADRA BUILDINGS ROSE UP from the edge of the narrow plateau to which the city clung, like barnacles to the upturned hull of an old boat. It was a place built to keep people out and its messy, uneven silhouette cut a ragged shape into the moonlit sky. There were, according to the sketches and notes in Rafus's journal, only two ways into the city: a main gateway and a smaller side entrance. The rest of the perimeter was either almost sheer cliff face or a scree of razor-sharp flint. There would be no sneaking into this place.

Haden, Decker and Sgt Blade first sighted Ghadra earlier in the day and they'd bivouaced, hidden in the trees, some miles away on the other side of the valley. The long hours until nightfall had been spent observing through the binoculars from a safe distance and they'd made a series of careful sorties to try and work out what system, if any, the Sardar used to change guards at the gates. There was none, as far as they could tell. Now, in the depths of the bone-cold night, it was time to make their move, to put their plan into action.

It had been Decker's idea that he and Haden should take on the role of Sardar agents, like the man who'd shadowed them from Chamat, and pretend to have been paid to bring in a 'captured' Quadrine spy. The idea might have been harder to sell during the day, but in the witching time it should, they all agreed, be much easier to bluff their way in. There was only one way to find out.

They came out of the darkness making no effort to hide their presence. Haden was leading, with Tybal asleep on his shoulder, and Decker at the rear; Blade, their 'prisoner', rode between them gagged and with her arms tied loosely behind her back. While each was playing a part, none of them had to pretend to be dog-tired and road weary. Haden kept waiting for some sign of being spotted by a watchman, but they'd almost reached the run-down building that served as the guardhouse for the city's less frequented side entrance before they were noticed.

Up ahead, some ten, twelve yards away, Haden finally saw movement behind one of the shuttered guardhouse windows, then a door banged open throwing out a shaft of tired lamp light, and a scrawny, bow-legged figure stumbled into view. Even from that distance Haden could see the guard had forgotten to put his gun in his holster.

'Halt!' The man's thin, reedy command was followed by the unmistakable sound of a yawn. 'Who goes there?'

Haden reined in his horse and jerked a thumb behind him. 'Got an escaped prisoner, a spy.'

A grunting noise came from inside the guardhouse.

The thin man cocked his head sideways. 'Says they gotta spy . . .'

More grunting.

''Ow should *I* know, Leck? I'm just saying what *they* said.' The guard yawned again and peered at them, pointing. 'That a parrot, mate?'

Haden nodded.

'It is? Right, thought so. Well, why've you come here, anyhow? This ain't the place t'bring prisoners in. Main gate's what you want.'

'Look,' Haden leant wearily on the pommel of his saddle, 'a gate's a gate, and we've been travelling for days, all through that storm – did you get that downpour here? We nearly drowned, me and my friend, looked like sewer rats. We just want to get the job finished – you going to make us traipse off somewhere else after all we've been through?'

'Leck!' The guard, yelled over his shoulder. 'Get yer fat behind out yer pit and give me an 'and, OK?'

Haden cursed under his breath. *Why* did this man have to be what his father had always called a 'by-the-book-or-not-at-all' type? He could feel the knot in his stomach tighten, a combination of exhaustion and annoyance making him ready to let rip; but the echo of his father's voice in his head made Haden stop, for a second imagining that he was watching him.

Think twice, he'd always said, *and act once*. Sten Akatine never lost his temper.

Taking a deep breath, Haden calmly dismounted. Carefully transferring Tybal to the pommel, he walked straight up to the guard – who, he was glad to see, was at least a couple of inches shorter than him and looking disconcerted.

Behind him he imagined Blade and Decker were wondering what he thought he was up to and, truth be told, he wasn't quite sure himself. It wasn't just that he was tired and wanted to get this thing over with, it was also that he needed to show Blade that he was worthy of his father's name and, face to face, he thought he might be able to convince the man to open the gate before his fat sidekick appeared. He stopped right in front of him.

'What?' The guard shrank back.

Grabbing the man by the scruff of his grimy tunic, Haden pulled him so close he could've counted the hairs on his unshaved chin, if he'd had the time and inclination.

'Open. The. Gate,' he whispered in his ear. 'Please?'

'*LECK?*' the man squeaked. '*HELP!*'

'Put 'im down.'

Haden turned to see the guardhouse doorway filled with the silhouette of a large, barrel-shaped, bald-headed man with no neck to speak of.

'I *said* "please" . . .' Haden tightened his grip on the guard.

'You won't go to the main gate, like you was told, then leave the prisoner 'ere and we'll deal wiv 'em,' the guard called Leck sniffed and wiped his nose on his sleeve. 'In the morning.'

'You going to pay me?' Haden enquired.

'In yer dreams.'

Haden felt the situation spinning out of his control, as if sand was running away through his fingers and he was all too aware that Blade and Decker were watching him fail. For a moment all he could think of doing was to shoot the two men and be done with it, but then he heard a even-tempered voice in his head, his father once again, saying *gold is quieter than a gun.*

He didn't have any gold in his pocket, but he did have silver.

'So how about *I* pay *you*?' Haden let the scrawny guard go and the man hacked dramatically, spat and massaged his throat. Turning to the second guard as he took out a small leather pouch, Haden shook it so the coins inside jingled . . .

The city slept like a drunk tramp – foul-smelling, noisy and fitful – and it was *nothing* like Jardesh. There were no wide streets, no paved squares and no fine buildings, the bleak moonlight casting impenetrable shadows that covered things probably best left hidden.

'Nicely done back there,' said Sgt Blade, untied and ungagged now they were out of sight of the gate. 'Thought for a moment you were going to try getting us in by shooting them.'

'It was close, but I thought I'd better save my bullets for when we really need them.'

'What we need now is to find somewhere to rest up.'

They were leading their horses through the narrow, roughly cobbled streets, followed by the sound of unseen vermin squabbling over discarded and festering pickings. The night breeze carried with it a lingering odour of over-cooked vegetables and turned milk.

'This place . . .' Decker wrinkled his nose. 'Like a pigsty.'

'Enjoy it while the streets are empty,' muttered Blade. 'Wait till sunrise and the pigs wake up,'

'Look,' Haden pointed ahead. 'Something's open down there. Might be an inn.'

'If it is,' said Decker, 'then I'm going to sleep with the horses.'

 **17** FIRST STEPS

'MOWLER!'

Mowler, who had fallen asleep at the table, his face in a plate of cold stew, sat up as if he'd had a pin stuck in him; congealing fat and gravy dripped down his cheek and nose and he couldn't open his right eye.

'Yes, uncle! Yes, I'm here! What . . . where?' Mowler wiped at the thick, greasy residue, looking round to see where his uncle's voice was coming from.

'Over here!'

Mowler finally saw Esquabar, his be-goggled head just visible at the top of the staircase, and he got up from the table a little unsteadily. 'I'm coming . . .'

'I need you downstairs. Now!'

Choosing the cleanest of the dirty cloths in the sink,

Mowler wiped the worst of the mess off his face, swallowed a couple of mouthfuls of tepid water and stretched his cramped muscles. He didn't know how long he'd slept but it really had not been long enough.

'*Mowler!*'

'I'm coming, I'm coming . . .'

At the bottom of the stairs he turned right, walking away from the rooms where the Transmute Engine sat cooling down, and saw his uncle hunched over a desk, scribbling furiously on a pad of paper.

Still lying on its sturdy wooden trestles was the rocket, all eight yards of it. It didn't look like much, but then everything that mattered was on the inside. Under the thin metal skin, cradled by the complex interior framework, was the *other* engine they'd built. The one that was supposed to (if nothing went wrong – and when had *that* ever been the case with Uncle Pero?) propel this missile up into the sky and send it crashing down on some poor, unsuspecting city in one of the Territories. Such were the dreams of his mad uncle . . .

'I'm here, what d'you want me to do?'

Esquabar looked round and tucked the pencil behind his ear. 'Help me to check this thing is ready to be brought upright.'

'Are we finished?'

'As finished as we'll ever be, Mowler, as we'll ever be . . .' Esquabar bent down and picked up a wrench, throwing it in Mowler's general direction. 'Check every nut, bolt and rivet.'

Mowler fumbled the catch and the wrench clanged on the floor. 'Who's going to help us get it vertical?'

'No one . . . that's what pulleys were invented for. Don't want riff-raff down here, poking their noses around.'

Mowler retrieved the wrench and started work. 'When are we going to test run the engine?'

'The maiden flight,' Esquabar slapped the side of the rocket, 'will be the test run.'

Mowler's jaw dropped, his eyebrows leapt up as if spring loaded and whatever words he was attempting to say couldn't quite get out of his mouth.

'We will only have *one* chance, nephew, and it *will* work – trust me.'

Mowler stared at his mother's older brother, who'd gone back to his scribbling. Trust? *Trust*? The more he thought about it, the more he was sure pigs had a better chance of flying before this tin tube did! One spark in the wrong place and the fuel – a completely unpredictable mix of liquid and powdered Phyre – would send them to kingdom come . . .

Two hours later Mowler had checked 'every nut, bolt and rivet', as instructed. He'd also attached all the ropes needed to raise the missile up off the trestles and onto its legs in readiness for getting it out of the building the following morning.

Fifteen minutes after the trap doors in the ceiling had

been opened, he and his uncle were standing back and admiring the rocket, which was now pointing proudly skyward. Its journey through ninety degrees, which Mowler had assumed on past evidence would be a hair-tearing nightmare of near disasters and nail-biting, turned out to have been simplicity itself. And the rocket was, Mowler couldn't help but admit, a magnificent sight.

'And now, the finishing touches!'

'What are they?' Mowler's shoulders and arms ached, in fact there wasn't a part of his body that didn't.

'Some colour . . .' Esquabar got the notepad off the table and showed Mowler a very precisely annotated pencil drawing of the upright rocket. 'Two coats should do it – everything you'll need is over there.'

While his uncle took a couple of panels off the rocket and began tinkering with the engine, Mowler got everything ready to paint the nose cone a bright red. As soon as that was done he began to carefully stencil the letters 'D' and 'U' and the numeral '1' down the side of the body, also in red.

'Perfect!' Esquabar declared when Mowler had finished the job, a slightly mad grin on his tired and deeply lined face. '*Ab*solutely perfect – if that idiot Usshien can read, he'll like that.'

18 FOUND AND LOST

THE INN HAD TURNED out to be full, leaving Haden and Sgt Blade with no choice but to join Decker and the horses and bed down in the stables as well. It hadn't been a particularly comfortable night, what was left of it, for anyone apart from Tybal.

After a bar-room breakfast, which filled their stomachs the way lead filled a mould, Blade slouched back in her chair and scanned the room. The place had emptied out and there was no one within earshot of the table they were sitting around.

She leant forward conspiratorially. 'We have a problem.'

'You mean apart from being in Ghadra under false pretences?' Haden held out a crust of bread for Tybal, perched behind him on the chair back, which the parrot thanked him for. 'From what I've seen, the way we look lets us fit in like we were born here.'

Blade shook her head. 'It's not that. This entire city's a thieves' kitchen and even if we *had* a room to put anything of value in,' she glanced at the pile of saddlebags on the floor between her and Decker, 'it wouldn't be safe to leave them for five minutes.'

'Take 'em with us?' suggested Decker.

'Asking for trouble.' Blade pushed her plate away. 'Someone's going to have to stay with them all the time. We'll have a rota, change every couple of hours. Only way to do it.'

'Just sit here?' Decker looked questioningly at Haden.

'We'll all have the bird for company,' Blade stood up. 'Right, bird?'

'*I think I'm going insane . . .*'

'Out of the mouths of babes and parrots.' Blade cracked a smile. 'Who's coming with me first?'

Decker had lost the toss of a decima and reluctantly taken the first stretch of looking after Tybal and the saddlebags. Pistols and knives in plain sight – like everyone else in Ghadra – Haden and Blade exited the inn and lost themselves in the crowded streets.

Haden had never seen so many people in one place before; had never had to deal with chaos on such a scale. It was noisy. It stank. It was totally overwhelming and, while he did his best to hide the innate fear welling up in his gut, he could tell by the way Blade was looking at him that he wasn't doing a very good job of it.

Everywhere people streamed this way and that, some loaded up like mules, others cajoling and cursing the real mules that were piled with even more things. There were men pulling carts, horses pulling wagons, grimy, ragged children darting about like fleas on the back of a cat and roving groups of heavily armed soldiers, some on horseback.

Sardar.

Haden had felt physically sick the first time he'd spotted their blood-red bandanas and dark blue facial tattoos, forced to turn away not only because he hated the sight of their swaggering arrogance, but also because he was sure his hatred would've have been all too plainly written on his face.

After about half an hour of trudging through the maze-like streets he grabbed Blade's arm and stopped her. 'What are we looking for?'

'Not sure.'

'Not *sure*?'

'I'll know when I see it . . .'

An hour or so later Blade still hadn't seen anything that seemed to interest her, but Haden had begun to realise he was getting more used to his new surroundings, which included having to be endlessly vigilant; given half a chance the children appeared capable of stealing even the clothes off your back. He had just fended off a devious attempt to relieve him of his dagger when Blade came to a sudden halt and knelt down to tie her bootlaces.

'See that?' she muttered.

'What?'

'Down this street.'

Haden glanced the way Blade had nodded and saw nothing out of the ordinary, certainly nothing they hadn't seen in every other street they'd been down: hordes of people, animals, bustle and shouting. He shrugged.

'Those big cart horses – the wagon-and-four down there.'

'What about it?'

'I've seen the wagon master before. I'm pretty sure he was part of the caravan I was travelling with when I got caught at the smelting works.'

Haden was still trying to figure out why any of this was worth mentioning when Blade stood up.

'Go and take a look, I'll be down at that tavern,' she pointed behind him and began walking away.

'But . . . ?'

'Can't risk him recognising me,' said Blade over her shoulder as she kept on walking. 'Don't be long . . .'

Haden snaked his way through the sluggish flow of people. His mother had always claimed to have eyes in the back of her head when he was a child and now he wished that *he* had them so he could really be as all-seeing as she had pretended to be. Right now, pushing his way down this dirty, crowded street, he felt increasingly alone and vulnerable with every step.

As he neared the wagon, moving past the enormous workhorses, sparks flying up from the cobble stones as they impatiently stamped steel-shod hooves the size of boulders, he began looking for a place where he could watch without being seen. Not easy in this rats' nest of a city.

Then, across the way he saw the dark oblong of a recessed doorway, tall enough that it *might* mean there were steps up to the actual door itself. Haden worked his way across to it and found that his luck was in, for now. Slipping out of the crowd, he moved up a couple of the worn stone steps and back into the shadows; from there he was safely able to look out across the moving river of heads and see what was happening on a narrow part of the other side of the street.

From his hiding place Haden could see a young man, pale and quite haggard, a pair of goggles pushed up on his head and wearing a leather apron over a dirty, off-white coat and he was arguing with an older, much bigger man. Although he couldn't hear what was being said, Haden knew the younger man was angry, his face screwed up, teeth bared like a rabid dog. If the wild gestures were anything to go by, it was all about something inside the building (thumb jerked savagely backwards) that any *idiot* could see was far bigger, possibly taller (one hand stretched as high as the younger man could make it go) than would fit on the *stupid* wagon (finger jabbing like a wasp's sting).

Apparently the older man did not agree that any of this (arms held up and then spread out wide) was *his* fault (large forefinger pointed insistently at his own chest), so the younger man (forefinger placed right on younger man's apron and pushed, hard) had better watch what he said, or (spit on the ground) else.

Haden noticed that there were four, maybe five hefty men hanging round, watching this difference of opinion, mildly amused expressions on their faces as they glanced at each other. The younger man, who seemed oblivious to the fact that he was completely outnumbered by people twice his size, did not take kindly to being pushed. Two red spots appeared on his pale cheeks and his eyes widened – *these people were going to see* (finger viciously shaken)! No one else in the street gave the altercation a moment of their time, but Haden found it fascinating.

Then the large door to the building behind the younger man opened slightly and someone else, dressed in much the same way – goggles, leather apron – came out. He was older, much taller, with a lined, hawk-like face, and he gently moved the younger man (his assistant?) out of the way and stood in front of the wagon master. For a moment he did nothing, just adjusted the pencil he had stuck behind his ear and stared at the man as if he was something vaguely unpleasant he'd stepped in. Then he leaned towards him and whispered in his ear, stood back and raised one eyebrow, waiting for a reply of some sort.

Whatever the tall man had said, it certainly got a reaction. Within minutes the wagon and crew were on their way, moving as if they had imps snapping at their heels. Haden stayed in the shadows, watching the tall man and his assistant as they watched the wagon move off; they both looked dog tired, like they hadn't slept in days, and he wondered what they were doing inside the building.

There was definitely something about them that didn't fit: they were different, out of place and, from what little he'd seen of Ghadra, were outsiders. This thought made Haden move down a step. If these two were strangers could the taller of the two men be the 'sciencer' Pero Esquabar, about whom both the spy and Rafus had talked? Maybe Haden's luck was in and he'd stumbled on him. He supposed it was possible, the city wasn't *that* big a place. But he'd never find out if he was right or not skulking in shadows, there was only one way to do that.

Haden walked down the steps and back out into the confused riptide of people, pushing his way across the street and making it to the other side as the tall man was about the open the door to go back inside the building. Haden dithered for a second, then tapped the shoulder of the younger man he was standing behind.

'I'm, um, I'm looking for work,' he said.

'You're what?' The younger man turned and frowned at him; he was, Haden realised, now he saw him up close, not that much older than Haden.

'I need a job.' Haden hoped he looked needy, yet useful.

'Really?' the boy looked at him wearily. 'Let me just check . . . Uncle Pero – do we need any help?'

'Don't be *stupid!*' The older man didn't even bother to look over his shoulder as he spoke, opening the door and disappearing inside the building, the words 'Come on, Mowler, we have work to do!' escaping just as the door slammed shut.

'I think that was "no".' Mowler grinned tightly at Haden, then followed after his uncle.

Haden stood looking at the door as it slammed shut in front of him, then heard a couple of bolts being engaged and a lock thrown. He stayed where he was for a moment or two, smiling in quiet disbelief that he actually *had* found Pero Esquabar; but what was he doing behind those doors? And would it be worth him hanging round to try and find out? Probably not, was the answer he came up with. What he *should* do was go and find Sgt Blade and tell her what he'd discovered and see what *she* thought they should do.

But, when he got back to the inn where she'd said she'd be waiting, he could find no sign of her.

19   Taken Away

Haden's first thought was that he must've gone to the wrong inn. But he hadn't. After five minutes of careful searching (he did not want to call attention to himself by appearing in any way frantic) there was no doubt that she wasn't there. Anywhere.

Back outside on the street Haden tried to work out what he should do next – stay where he was for a bit longer, in case Blade turned up? Or go to where Decker was waiting and talk things over with him? Because two heads, as his mother had always said, were better than one. Which at that moment had to be true, as he couldn't make his mind up either way.

In the end he decided there was only one thing to do. Digging into his pocket, Haden found a small silver coin and flicked it in the air: heads he stayed, tails he went. He watched the shiny disc spin, almost in slow motion in the dusty air, and then, as he went to catch it, another hand appeared out of nowhere. Like a snake's tongue (this hand, oddly, only had two fingers), it snatched the tumbling coin as it fell. Haden only just managed to grab the wizened owner of the hand before she lost herself in the crowds.

'You!' Haden pushed the ragged individual up against the inn wall. 'Give it back, you thieving bandit!'

'Young sir, please sir, don't hit a poor crone, sir! Don't batter me to pieces for the sake of such a *tiny* silver thing that's as thin as a baker's excuse! No sir, please sir, don't sir! I didn't mean nothing, strike me down if I did. It was all a dreadful mistake, it was the bad person we *all* has inside of us that did it, sir . . .'

Ignoring the torrent of words and excuses, which showed no sign of stopping, Haden kept one hand on his captive's bony shoulder and looked her up and down. She was a small weasel of a woman with thin, grey hair that dribbled out from under her mobcap in greasy curls, her prominent front teeth were stained a yellowy-brown and dirt was ingrained deep in her weathered skin. She stared back at Haden through small, deceitful eyes that twitched incessantly. And, there was no doubt about it, she smelled like a weasel as well.

'I'm a frail pretence, I am, sir, not worthy of your time, not worth the bother of bothering with or hurting, *especially* hurting, really I'm not, sir. What good could it possibly serve to play like a cat with a brittle-boned wretch such as myself? Know what I mean? I'm sure you do, intelligent young sir like yourself. You and your friend, what you're waiting for with the patience of a *saint*, must have more important things to do, I'm sure, you have that look . . .'

'What did you say?'

'Me? About what, sir? When?'

'Just now, about my friend, the one you supposed I was waiting for.'

'I did . . . did I?' Shrugging, the old woman rolled her eyes, attempted a winning smile and failed. 'I don't remember much from one minute to the next no more, sir, got the brain of a spud, sir, really I have. Hardly know *what* I'm saying . . .'

His father's slim-bladed dagger appeared in Haden's free hand, its point nestling in a fold of skin in the old woman's plucked-chicken throat.

'Maybe I can help. Let a little blood,' Haden poked with the blade slightly, the old woman winced and a tiny scarlet bead rolled down her neck, 'to clear your head. Know what *I* mean? Who are you, anyway?'

'Me? I'm nobody, a worthless *particle*, sir, like what gets scraped off of a shoe before it gets to go on into a house.'

'Even dust has a name. What's yours?'

'*My* name?' A look of total confusion passed like a cloud over the old woman's pinched face. 'Well, truth be told, and if you want the full and complete testimony, sir – which, by the look on your face, you do – it's Jacatha Hestor Boullian Matchlock. On me sainted mother's grave, sir, that's the name I got give, but I ain't been called by that label for more years than . . .'

'Fine, fine,' Haden growled. 'What *do* they call you, then?'

'Match, sir. "Do-this-do-that Match" is what I go by, and what I do – some of this and a bit of that . . .'

'Put a cork in it, Match, and do this: just tell me what happened to my friend.'

'She got took.'

'Took?'

Match started to nod, but stopped when it made the blade dig in harder.

'Who by?'

'Dunno . . .' Match, for whom lying was like breathing, saw the look in Haden's eyes. 'I mean to say, put it like this: I don't know them *personally*, do I? But I would be prepared to hazard a guess that they was Usshien's men. By the looks of them, what with the tattoos and all.' Match lowered her voice. 'I *hate* them Sardar, sir – this was a nice, quiet place before they started with all their marauding and pillage.'

'Shut up, Match.' Haden sheathed his dagger and dragged the raggedy figure off down the street with him. 'You're coming with me.'

'Me, sir, why, sir? Is it the money? I was only trying to help, sir, thought you'd dropped it – look, here it is!'

Match shoved her right hand out, the silver coin held between a thumb and one of her two fingers. 'See? You can let me go now sir . . .'

'Keep the money.'

'*Keep* it?' Match tripped over her own feet and would have fallen if Haden hadn't still got her by the scruff of the neck.

'Play your cards right, you could earn some more. Maybe enough to afford a bath . . .'

Decker turned back and leant his elbows on the bar. He sniffed, his nose wrinkling.

'I know,' Haden nodded, looking across the room at their table where a very nervous Match now sat, watched by Tybal. 'She smells.'

'Why'd you bring her here? And where's Blade?'

'The old woman says some Sardar appeared out of nowhere and took her off.'

'So what're we going to do about getting her back?'

'Don't think there's a lot we *can* do, just the two of us.' Haden paid for the three glasses of murky ale a bar boy had set down next to him, then picked up two of them. 'Match told me she heard one of the soldiers who dragged Blade off call her a spy, so someone must've recognised her. She said they've likely taken Blade to what she called the Draka – it's like a fortified building, with a gaol. And she said *draka* was a Sardar word that means "no exit".'

Decker picked up his glass. 'We have to try, don't we? I mean, we can't leave her there!'

Haden shook his head; he'd had time to think this through, think about the situation the way he hoped his father would have done, and he'd come to the conclusion that a rescue attempt was probably not what they should be planning. Not now.

'I think we're going to have to leave her, for the moment.'

'But . . . !'

'Tell me why we came here, Deck! Listen, we came to get information, find out about what Usshien's up to and finish the mission Rafus was on, right? Like he asked us to. We *can't* do anything about Blade right now – my father always used to say you should finish one job before you started another. And I think he'd say I was right about this.' Haden looked at Decker, his friend staring into his glass of cloudy ale. 'What do *you* say, Deck?'

Decker glanced up, his lips pursed, a frown creasing his forehead.

'Don't like it, Haden, not one bit,' he sighed and shrugged his shoulders, 'though I can see the sense. But what's going to happen with the bags?'

Haden nodded at Match. 'That's what *she's* here for.'

'Her? I wouldn't trust her as far as you could throw her!'

'Don't have to. I've got an idea, so, whatever I tell her, you back me up, all right?'

Decker nodded in agreement, but still wore the troubled frown on his face.

'Good news is, I *have* found Esquabar.'

'You did?' Decker lost the frown. 'Where?'

'Tell you in minute, after we sort this out . . .' Haden sat down at the table. 'Listen carefully, my rancid little friend,' he put a glass in front of Match, 'because if you don't do *exactly* what I tell you, I *will* know.'

Match's eyes twitched and skittered as she looked from Haden to Decker. Nervousness made her hands shake so much that she spilt quite a bit of ale onto her ragged skirts.

'What you, um, ah . . . what you want me t'do?'

'Sit right there, drink the ale I've bought you, eat the food I *shall* buy you and guard our bags like you owned them. Do *not* move out of that chair. D'you understand, Match?'

Match's head nodded in a way that looked it was halfway to a confused shake.

'And like I said, I *will* know if you don't follow these instructions to the letter.'

Match's eyes darted sideways before she could stop herself.

Haden followed where she'd glanced. 'The people here, they don't care what you do. But he does.'

'He?' Match's eyes twitched manically. 'Who?'

'The parrot.'

Tybal, asleep on the back of a chair, chose that moment to open an eye and stare at Match.

'He may not look like it, but he's the necromancer we work for. One of his enemies somehow managed to change him into a bird,' Haden turned to Decker. 'Bad magic, right Deck?'

'The worst,' Decker sucked in his breath and shook his head. '*Never* seen the like before.'

'Our master,' Haden bowed slightly in Tybal's direction, 'heard there was another 'mancer here in Ghadra, so we came to see if he could help undo the spell.'

Match hunched forward elbows on her knees and one eye on Tybal. 'You mean wosisname, that Esquabar? Where you was this morning? Talk about bad magic!'

'*How* long were you following me, Match?' Haden tensed, annoyed with himself for not noticing.

'Just a little. Moments, or maybe minutes, possibly minutes – not what *I* would call a *long* time, sir!' Match wound her fingers into a tangle under Haden's stern gaze. 'More likely it was a bit, sir, just a bit of time. And not really *following*, more like . . .'

Haden leaned across the table. 'Be quiet, Match. What d'you know about Esquabar? And remember, our master is listening to *everything* you say.'

'Don't know much, sir – may I be struck down if that's not the truth,' Match looked over at Tybal. 'But ever since he come here there've been accidents, terrible, *loud* accidents, sir! There's been explosions and people killed an' all. Only Sardar, but still . . . they had to scrape a couple of them off the wall, on my life they did, sir.

Heaven alone knows what dark and hellish dealings goes on in there, sir, Heaven alone.'

Haden finished his ale and stood up. 'We'll be back to check on you, Match, so make sure you're where you should be.' He bowed to Tybal, Decker following suit. 'Goodbye, master, we will do our best.'

The parrot, awake now, made it's own bowing movement back; watching everything, Match's little eyes were out on stalks.

'*I think I'm going insane* . . .' said Tybal in Theraston Mykram's quavering voice. '*Help me!*'

Match went rigid with fear.

'You will be yourself again soon, master.' Haden had to look away in case Match saw him smiling.

20   Out of the Frying Pan

'WHAT WAS THAT YOU were saying to me?' Pero Esquabar flicked backwards and forwards through a well-thumbed notebook, then stopped at a particular page and looked up at his nephew as he retrieved the pencil from behind his ear. 'Out there . . . something about help?'

'Nothing. Somebody asking if there was a job. They were looking for work.'

'More likely they'd been sent here by Usshien to spy on us!'

'He didn't look like a Sardar,' Mowler sagged like an unstarched collar and sighed, which came out much louder than he'd intended.

'What's the matter?'

'Just thinking how nice it would be to have help, an extra pair of hands.'

'Too risky, *far* too risky! And anyway, we've nearly finished – as soon as those idiots get back with the right wagon we can get the rocket out of here and over to the launch site. Now, where was I . . .'

Mowler watched his uncle, nose back in his notebook, stride off, nearly collide with a table and disappear back downstairs into the basement. There was no doubting the man was a genius – the evidence was everywhere, from the towering shape of the rocket's nose cone poking through the floor to the Transmute Engine and what it had produced – but he definitely had his failings.

For one thing, he rarely thought things through to their logical conclusion, and for another he *hated* being told he was wrong or might have made a mistake. Mowler had seen from the start that there would be problems if they built the rocket in the basement; it may well have been fairly easy to get it standing upright, but just wait until they had to manoeuvre it out of the building! Past experience had taught him that there was no use in pointing these things out (unless he wanted to risk getting a good clip round the ear), as once Esquabar had made up his mind how to do something, that was generally how it was done. No matter what.

Well, he thought as he slouched across to the stairs, the chickens were going to come home to roost today when they attempted to get a 'team' of bone-headed, pea-brained navvies to winch the rocket onto the wagon without breaking it. All he could be thankful for was that the fuel store was already at the launch site and under heavy guard, which meant that getting it into the rocket's tanks was a problem somewhat further down a rather long list of Things To Do Before Mowler Died.

They had worked solidly for hours, though there still seemed to Mowler that there were quite a lot of loose ends. But at least the rocket was finally out of the basement, so after they'd eaten there was no reason they shouldn't get a few hours of precious, delicious sleep. That was the plan, or had been until out of the blue Uncle Pero had derailed.

'What?' Mowler blinked slowly, hardly able to believe what he'd just heard his uncle say. Part of him assumed that extreme tiredness must be making the man hallucinate. He sat staring across the table, his jaw slack, a piece of gravy-soaked bread halfway to his mouth. 'You want to do *what*?'

'Pack up and leave Ghadra now . . .' Esquabar hissed, looking round as if there might possibly be people hiding in the shadows, listening. 'It's the *only* thing to do. The plan's not going to work, and that maniac will kill me – *us*.'

'How d'you know the plan won't work! It's only going to happen once – we can't *test* it!'

'It's a stupid, stupid, *stupid* plan, I can see that now!

We should just take the gold and diamonds and make a run for it . . .' Esquabar stood up dramatically, his chair flying backwards and tipping over with a crash.

'Uncle, wait a minute! Think . . .' Mowler rushed round the table and grabbed his uncle's arm. 'Do you suppose Usshien trusts you?'

'Me?' Esquabar looked shocked at being asked such a patently ludicrous question. 'Of course not! He doesn't trust *any*body!'

'Exactly.'

'Exactly what do you mean by "exactly"?' Esquabar frowned.

'I mean that, beyond a shadow of a doubt, this place is being watched night and day. We try and make a run for it and we won't make to the end of the next street, let alone out of the city gates.' Mowler picked up his uncle's chair and sat him back down on it, pulling over a second chair for himself. 'Don't worry, it's a *good* plan, really it is! You know Usshien, there's no way that evil little man will want anyone else firing the rocket. He'll be the one to throw the switch, guaranteed.'

Mowler thought he'd done a terrific job of sounding very much more confident than he felt on the inside, because he sort of agreed with his uncle. It wasn't a very good plan because, as usual, it hadn't been properly thought through. A large part of its success relied on a couple of barrels of Phyre detonating on cue – which, seeing as ever since Esquabar had invented the stuff they'd had their work cut out *stopping* it from doing just that, was not going to be a problem. The problem lay in how *they* were supposed to get away before the Phyre exploded and killed Usshien. If they had the whisker of a chance of doing that Mowler believed it must be the tiniest whisker imaginable.

What he now had to do (on top of everything else) was stop his uncle from coming up with any more idiotic ideas. Because attempting to do a moonlight flit truly would be like leaping out of the frying pan and straight into a barrel of Phyre . . .

21 UP ON THE ROOF

AFTER FIRST CHECKING THE ominous and heavily fortified Draka, where they presumed Sgt Blade was being held, just to confirm there was no chance of a rescue attempt, Haden and Decker had spent the rest of the day observing Esquabar's building.

They'd witnessed the long and extremely drawn-out process by which a huge metal dart, the pointed end painted a bright, shiny red, had eventually been brought out and laboriously strapped onto a massive horse-drawn wagon. They'd then watched chaos ensue as a wheel had sheared off one of the axles. Esquabar and his assistant had nearly had a fit when that'd happened.

They still didn't know what the dart was, or what it might be for, but they knew *where* it was. Decker had followed the wagon and watched as it was hauled upright on its four 'legs' and tethered to a large stone platform in the middle of some wasteland at the very edge of the city.

But they still had no idea what they should be doing about it.

A problem which Blade might have solved, had she been with them.

One thing Haden and Decker *had* learned was that other people were watching Esquabar, and they weren't trying to hide the fact. There were two men covering the front of the building and another the back, but they were bored, idle and feckless and never noticed that they themselves were being watched.

It was now well after dusk. Decker had just left to go back to the inn to check on Match and Tybal when Haden noticed that the lookout at the rear had fallen asleep. Seizing this opportunity, and using the deep shadows as cover, Haden had found a way of getting himself up onto the roof of an abandoned house opposite Esquabar's building.

From his fairly precarious position (the roof had more holes in it than his long-dead grandfather's socks) Haden now had a clear line of sight over the high wall surrounding the property. Only the windows on the upper floors had been shuttered so, using Rafus's binoculars, he could see right into the ground floor, which was, anyway, where most of the activity seemed to be taking place. Lights were burning in every room so he could see Esquabar and his young assistant and watch what they were doing. And, if he was any judge, it looked very much like they were packing up and getting ready to move. Did that mean they'd finished whatever they'd come to Ghadra to do?

Then Haden saw something which nearly made him lose his footing and plummet through a gaping hole in the roof. He'd watched Esquabar and the boy stagger in with two small, but obviously very heavy crates and dump them down on a table. The real surprise came when they opened up the first crate and Haden saw the unmistakable amber-yellow glow of . . . gold! Gold – and a *lot* of it, from the way they'd carried those boxes. Was this what Esquabar had been paid to make the great big metal thing they'd watched being taken out earlier in the day? It seemed like far too much though what, thought Haden, did *he* know about business transactions?

But when he saw Esquabar open a couple of fair-sized pouches, pouring some of their contents – mostly pea-sized chunks of glittering ice – into the palm of his hand, Haden knew something out of the ordinary was going on. The only diamonds he'd ever seen were the rough, uncut ones drunk prospectors had occasionally shown off in the bars back in Starpoint, so he knew what he was looking at. And here was a man with fistfuls of the things.

There must be enough for *ten* kings' ransoms in that room!

Was it stolen? If it was then the only person it could possibly be stolen *from* was Usshien. Surely Esquabar couldn't have robbed Usshien. Could he? Was that why he was getting ready to go? And did Usshien suspect what had happened – was *that* why there were guards outside the building? Yet more unanswered questions to add to all the others.

After Esquabar and his boy had repacked the gold and diamonds in a number of leather satchels and taken them away, Haden couldn't see where, they'd put out all the lights. Haden was left staring at the darkened, mysterious house wondering about the scene he'd just witnessed. He was jerked out of his reverie by an owl hooting – Decker's signal that he was in the vicinity. Haden replied in kind and carefully began inching his way back down to street level, his head a jumble of wild, unruly thoughts.

Haden awoke from yet another night spent in the hay loft, hauled, unwillingly, from his dream by an ungodly hubbub from outside the stables. Crawling over to the one window in the loft, he found it was so filthy he couldn't see anything. If he wanted to find out what the fuss was all about, he was going to have to go downstairs. Shuffling back to where he'd slept to get his boots, past a snoring Decker, with Tybal perched above him on a rafter, he saw a tightly curled-up ball of rags. It looked as if a giant, ill-kempt dormouse had crept in and nested with them, until he remembered that Match had pleaded to be allowed to sleep under a roof, even offering to pay for the privilege with some of her earnings. It had, she claimed, been years since she'd had that simple luxury. They hadn't made her pay, but they had insisted she had a wash. Though, in the stables, that hadn't made an awful lot of difference.

On the street it was pandemonium. Haden, who thought Ghadra had been an extraordinary sight the day before, was staggered by what he saw now. The whole city seemed to be on the move, a tide of humanity sweeping past the inn, whooping and hollering like excited children. He tried asking passers by what it was all about, but no one wanted to stop and chat, so he forced his way against the flow and made it into the bar-room where a solitary, disgruntled waitress stood cleaning glasses with a damp cloth.

'What's that all about?' Haden indicated behind him. 'D'you know?'

'S'down at the Flats . . .' the girl brushed hair off her face with the back of her hand. 'Some kind of show, they say, to watch this new machine Usshien's got – they moved it down there yesterday, din't you see? Big thing, it was.'

'Right, down at the Flats, thanks . . .'

'I can't go, which ain't fair as why should I have to stay here when there's not going to be any custom, right? Specially as they say a spy's going to be executed as well. A proper event that's going to be.' The girl spat in the glass she was holding and gave it a final, cursory wipe. When she looked up, Haden had gone.

22 NO SECOND CHANCE

'Is it finished?'

'Final preparations are being made, as we speak, sir.' Esquabar forced himself to bow slightly in Dasmed Usshien's general direction.

'If this doesn't work . . .' Usshien let the threat hang in the air, like a vulture over a dying man, as he paced round the dank room. Then he stopped. 'Well, what're you waiting for? Get out of here and make sure that weapon is ready! I shall be arriving at noon.'

'Noon . . .' Esquabar repeated, backing away. That gave him little more than two hours to make sure everything was completed. 'I, ah, I look forward to it.'

'And have you heard?' Usshien said, just as Esquabar reached the door.

'Heard?' Esquabar stopped, furiously attempting to remember what Usshien had said to him the last time they'd met.

'That spy I was telling you about? We caught her . . .' Without any kind of warning Usshien took out his pistol and fired at a bottle on a nearby sideboard, causing an eruption of glass and wine. The noise was deafening in the confined space and the bullet whined as it ricocheted off the stone wall, making Esquabar duck. 'So, I'm combining your demonstration with an execution!'

Hurrying down the corridor Esquabar could still hear Usshien's slightly crazed giggle as he loosed off a couple more shots. The man was a complete and utter lunatic! A psychopath! He was going to make Mowler *swear* – if they got out of this place with the skin still on their backs – never, *ever* to let him do anything like this again. In fact he was going to give the boy permission, in writing, to lock him up for his own good if at any time in the future it looked like he was about to do anything as stupid as this.

The heaving mass of spectators that had gathered on the Flats were in the mood for entertainment; this despite the fact that armed Sardar horsemen, with whips they weren't backward using, were maintaining some kind of order by randomly beating anyone who caught their attention. The party atmosphere was helped by the appearance of an increasing number of vendors who'd set up their stalls along the outer perimeter of the test site or were wandering through the crowds selling trinkets and a variety of things that just about passed for food and drink – if you were *very* thirsty, or ravenous.

Mowler, who was trying to get insubordinate and uncooperative navvies to do what he wanted simply by shouting at them, wished *he* had a whip. And a gun. And a horse. He stopped yelling for a moment. Actually, what he *really* wanted was to be somewhere, *any*where else than where he was, doing what he was. The curved, sandbag wall that Esquabar had told him to make sure was five-foot thick, eight-foot high and twelve-foot wide by the time he got back was almost complete. But not quite. Hence all the shouting.

Behind this barricade was a large wooden work bench, complete with cupboards and drawers, on which sat the control switch that was connected by wire to the rocket's engine. Some thirty feet away, the rocket stood, magnificent on its stone podium, waiting, sun glinting off its polished metal skin. A few yards beyond it, the plateau ended in a precipitous cliff face which fell hundreds feet into a gorge below. Turning round where he stood Mowler swallowed dryly. If this all went wrong, they'd be trapped with no means of escape. A sheer drop on one side, a ravening crowd on the other, and him and Esquabar in the middle – with Usshien. It didn't bear thinking about.

Squaring his shoulders, Mowler tried to ignore all

the negative thoughts as he walked up to the person who claimed to be the foreman and tapped him on the shoulder.

'Do they,' he pointed to the labourers, 'understand that if that,' he pointed to the wall, 'isn't finished by the time Usshien gets here their lives won't be worth living?' He drew a finger sharply across his throat.

The foreman ignored him.

'Your funeral,' Mowler grumbled to himself, going back to check, one more time, that all the wiring was in place, all the connections secure and the ignition charges ready. They weren't going to have a second chance.

23 · DOWN AT THE FLATS

HADEN FOLLOWED DECKER, WHO was digging his way through the almost solid mass of people crammed onto the Flats using his elbows like pick-axes. Sardar horsemen were having their work cut out controlling the crowds and keeping them from pushing forward.

'The old woman,' stopping when he was just out of reach of the Sardar whips, Decker made space for Haden, 'd'you think . . .'

'I think Match *truly* believes Tybal is a 'mancer who's been turned into a parrot by bad magic. She'll be there when we get back, Deck, she's too scared not to be.' Haden squeezed himself in front of Decker, stood on tip-toes and scanned the area in front of him. Out beyond the rabble, to his right, on the curved, flat expanse of wasteland, was a thick wall of sandbags that had to be protecting something he couldn't see. To his left, at the far edge of the wide plateau, was the huge, pointed metal cylinder standing upright on its four legs. Haden could see a hatch had been removed from the body of the red-tipped 'dart' and Esquabar and his assistant were tinkering with whatever was inside.

'D'you think Blade's the spy they're going to execute?'

Haden nodded.

'How are we going to stop them?'

'I'll . . .'

Before Haden could finish what he was saying a loud roaring came from behind them.

'Can you see what's happening, Deck?'

'There's a lot of people on horseback – looks like someone's trying to make a way through.'

'Good luck to them.'

As soon as they realised who was approaching, a couple of mounted guards on the Flats began ordering the crowd to move, carving a space with their whips. Haden looked back at the big silver 'dart' and saw Esquabar stop what he was doing and run over to the bench behind the sandbag barricade. Then a whisper swarmed through the gathering like a nest of wasps on the move: Usshien had arrived.

Haden watched as the mob parted to let the Sardar leader through. He stared, his throat tightening, as he caught his first sight of the man responsible for the death of his family and friends and the destruction of his old life. He felt his mouth go dry and he realised that somehow his pistol had got into his hand. Then he felt Decker grip his shoulder.

'Careful.'

Haden took a deep, deep breath and slowly reholstered his gun.

Riding behind their leader came a large squad of armed riders and bringing up the rear were two more Sardar with a third person between them: a small, slight figure who was gagged, arms tied behind her back, someone who had been so badly beaten that it was hard to recognise her. As she rode by, Haden was almost sure Sgt Blade's eyes had caught his for a moment before she looked away.

Mowler was in pain. It was like someone was actually hammering nails into his skull. And he ached. All over. He was so tense he felt as if his muscles might begin to tear themselves apart, but there was no way he was going to be able to relax until this was all over, one way or the other; one way meaning they lived, the other that they died.

Everything was ready, there was nothing else he could do. It all now depended on Usshien – who had just made an appearance – demanding to be the one to launch the missile.

Esquabar had ordered Mowler to stay with the rocket

to ensure that the second part of the plan could be set in motion. Always assuming, of course, that the first part worked. As was the way with his uncle, there was no margin for error, no exit strategy, no 'what if?' factored in to any of his calculations. Which meant he'd never imagined there'd be so many people here to watch the proceedings and making escape under cover of panic an impossibility. Mowler looked longingly at the silhouettes of the birds wheeling so carelessly high up above him. What he wouldn't give for a pair of wings.

Usshien had now made it through the mob and was instructing two riders to bring a third over towards the rocket. This must be the spy Esquabar had told him was going to be executed. Mowler shook his head. These people were animals. No, they were worse than animals – he'd never heard of another creature that would treat the death of one of its own as entertainment. The thought of what was going to happen made him feel so sick he had to turn away and stare out across the surrounding peaks to try and calm himself. Not for the first time he was saddened that this awful place should have such beautiful views. It didn't seem right.

'Oi! Move it!'

Mowler spun round to find himself looking at two Sardar holding a badly beaten person between them. Something about the delicacy of the captive's jaw, the shape of the eyes maybe, alerted him to the fact that this was a woman, which, for some reason, came as a shock.

'What're you doing?'

'Orders,' one of the soldiers said. 'Gotta tie her up under this thing.' He nodded at the rocket.

'You can't!' Mowler spread his arms out in a quite useless *keep away!* gesture.

'Try and stop us and you'll end up under there with her, mate.'

24 NOW OR NEVER

HADEN HAD BEEN FEELING bad; cold, dark tentacles of anxiety and alarm spreading out from the pit of his stomach ever since he'd watched Blade ride past. Now, as he saw her being tied up underneath Esquabar's strange construction, he felt even worse. Surely there had to be *something* they could do to help her?

But the harder he tried to think, the less a rescue bid seemed possible. Haden bit his knuckle so hard he drew blood. He did *not* want to leave Ghadra with his tail between his legs, on the other hand a suicide mission was not going to achieve anything. It occurred to him that going out in a blaze of glory would just be failure cloaked in bravery, and if he and Decker died for a lost cause what a stupid waste of their lives that'd be.

Decker nudged Haden. 'What're we going to do?'

'Don't know, Deck. Wish I did.' Haden dug his hands deep in his pockets and shook his head. 'Been trying to think of something, but the two of us against the rest of the world? That's not going to work is it?'

Wracking his brains about what they could possibly do, Haden's fingers obsessively played with the leather cord he'd discovered in his pocket. As he concentrated it was like he'd disappeared into a bubble and what was happening around him got closed out.

Maybe one of them could cause some kind of disturbance, allowing the other the chance to get to Blade? Maybe . . . the cord had become knotted round one of his fingers . . . maybe he should go the whole hog and try and shoot Usshien, create some *real* mayhem . . . Decker nudged Haden again, bringing him back down to earth.

'We should go,' he muttered. 'I don't want to see what happens.'

'We can't just *leave* her, Deck!'

'You got a better idea?'

'Not really . . .' Haden shook his head as he pulled his hand out of his pocket and absentmindedly began unknotting the cord from his finger. He glanced down at the small, black pouch that was attached to the leather cord and almost put it back in his pocket. He blinked. Maybe he did have an idea after all, because, if he wasn't much mistaken, this was the pouch he'd got from Eloi back out in the wilderness.

The pouch that was full of powder.

Powder that could make you go crazy.

'I need a drink, you want one, Deck?'

Before Decker had a chance to answer, Haden was off, pushing his way towards a man selling some kind of refreshment from a battered metal tank strapped to his back.

'Give me a shot!' Haden waved his hand, proffering a coin he knew was too much and would get him served faster. He accepted a chipped glass two-thirds full of a dark yellow liquid and turned away, pretending to take a sip. Immediately he bent over, clutching his throat and spat loudly.

'Horse sweat! Are you selling *horse* sweat? Well you can have it back, mate, cos *I'm* not drinking it!' Haden surreptitiously emptied Eloi's demonic powder into the glass. Reaching out, he lifted the lid on the vendor's reservoir and poured the contents of the glass back in, slamming the lid shut.

'Why'd you do that?' Decker said as Haden pushed his way back through crowds.

'Wait and see . . .'

Pero Esquabar was horrified. In his mind an execution was synonymous with a firing squad: something, no matter how appalling, that would be over in a matter of seconds. A incident he could turn his back on, put his fingers in his ears and ignore. But this! He knew that he would never, not even in a *hundred* lifetimes, have come close to imagining the end that Usshien had in mind for the spy. He was having her tied up *under* the rocket so that when the engine was fired up, she'd burn to death. It was monstrous, but then this was the man who gave barbarians a bad name.

'It's past midday, Esquabar.'

Esquabar dragged his eyes away from what was going on over by the rocket and saw Usshien dismounting. He had a sudden, unavoidable need to yawn and turned his head away so the man wouldn't see him; he'd heard that fear made you yawn, and there was no denying he was frightened, but he didn't want to show Usshien how terrified he was.

'Everything's ready for you, sir.' Esquabar bowed so low his back hurt. 'This way.'

He led the diminutive figure behind the high, curved sandbag wall to the work bench, which was littered with tools, wires, leads, numerous boxes with dials, a small brazier used to heat a soldering iron and, at its centre, an impressively large lever with a couple of thick cables running off the back of the table top. Usshien was not to know this but everything, except the lever and its cables, was window dressing, designed to look 'scientific', 'technical' and as if it was the result of long nights of mental toil and physical labour. Even the lever was far bigger than it needed to be for the simple job it had to do.

'Do I pull this?' Usshien strode over towards the

table, his hand outstretched and Esquabar thought for a second he was going to faint.

'*No, sir!* No, I mean, yes – but not right now, not at this *exact* moment!'

'Why not?' Usshein scowled, his lip curling. 'You said it was all ready, didn't you?'

'I did, I did, sir, you're absolutely right, absolutely. I did . . .' Esquabar knew his eye was twitching and sweat was pouring off him in rivulets, but he prayed he just looked as if he'd been working like a dog. 'But I, um, I have to check *one last thing*, sir – just *one* last thing. I want this to be perfect.'

'It had better be, Esquabar.'

Mentally crossing everything he had, Esquabar walked away. Behind the bench's locked cupboard doors sat two medium-sized barrels, each three-quarters full of liquid Phyre, with a simple crossed-wire fuse inserted in each top. The wires were attached to a lead/ acid battery, and the battery was connected to the impressively large lever. When the lever was thrown the circuit would be completed. When the circuit was completed the crossed wires in the fume-filled space in each barrel would spark. When they did that – *BOOM!*

No more Dasmed Usshien.

In his mind's eye, Esquabar had imagined the Sardar leader being surrounded by his highest-ranking officers and the explosion killing them all, leaving the rest of the vile dog-pack leaderless and in a state of utter confusion. And then, so the scenario went, as soon as

Usshien had blown himself, and everyone of any importance, to smithereens, Mowler was supposed to fire up the rocket's engine. This, Esquabar imagined, would cause yet more chaos, during which they'd make a run for it back to the building. For good measure, after two or three minutes the rocket itself would then blow up instead of taking off and, under the cover of all the resulting mayhem, they would depart this loathsome city. With the gold and the diamonds.

Of course there were a number of things he hadn't foreseen. Like the seething mob of innocent bystanders (although, as residents of Ghadra, they couldn't be *that* innocent . . .) who might get killed, but would *definitely* make it impossible for them to get away before the rocket blew up. And then there was the spy, who was at this very moment being strapped down under the rocket.

'Mowler!' Esquabar waved as he broke into a trot. 'I need a word!'

The accusation that he was selling horse sweat hadn't seemed to bother the drink-seller or his customers, and in the noon-day heat Haden watched as the man continued to do a brisk trade. He had no idea how much of the powder Eloi had put in their water carriers to cause the reaction it did, but Haden hoped that the pouch had contained enough to produce some kind of effect. All he could do was wait and see.

He did not have to wait long.

Slowly at first, then, like straw catching fire, he saw the madness begin to take hold. People began to dribble and go cross-eyed, others twitched as if possessed and started to point and scream hysterically; vicious fights broke out as the unaffected became entangled with the deranged and soon trouble was breaking out in more and more places. Trouble that couldn't be put down with a whip or, as soon became apparent, a gun.

'How's this supposed to help?' Decker pushed away a man who was crying like an abandoned child as he frantically tore at some invisible horror on his arms.

'Who's going to be watching *us* now?' Haden shouted back above the rising clamour as a Sardar rider fired into the crowd moments before he was pulled screaming from his horse. 'It's now or never – let's go!'

25   The Last Chance

AT FIRST DASMED USSHIEN thought the roaring he could hear was the crowd's anticipation of what was to come – he knew he could always keep them happy with a good execution. As he carefully inspected the paraphernalia on the bench in front of him, he imagined the awesome, magnificent sight of the rocket taking off – *his* rocket, his great weapon, his way of controlling more Territories than any one man ever had! He knew that this was a day that would be talked about for years to come. He was sure of it.

Then a shot rang out.

Usshien whirled around to find himself staring at a scene straight out of a nightmare; it was as if a rift had opened up in the ground and spewed out fire-pit demons and other hellish creations. Which couldn't happen. Not today. Today was *his* day!

'Guards!' Usshien yelled, pulling out his heavy, blued-steel pistol. 'Guards – to me!'

But no one heard him, or if they did, they didn't pay him any attention, and that didn't make *any* sense. Could there be anyone who didn't realise the consequences of ignoring him? He would *not* be ignored! Turning back to the bench, determined he would have everyone's attention, Usshien grabbed the lever and pulled it down. In the split second it took for the connection to be made and the tiny, insignificant sparks to crackle into life in the barrels, one corner of Usshein's mouth moved fractionally upwards.

The half-smile died, along with its owner, in an intense, fiery surge of heat, white light and thunderous sound that punched out from a point underneath the bench, atomising everything around it: blasting a hole in the barricade; turning sand into glass; digging a smoking crater twelve-feet wide and six-feet deep in the plateau.

As the final rumbling echo from the surrounding mountains faded away to nothing, an odd, whistling silence fell on the shocked survivors.

Haden picked himself up. He couldn't hear anything but a high-pitched whine in his ears as he staggered about, unable to maintain his balance properly as he tried to find Decker in the devastation. Completely disoriented, Haden didn't know where he was and for a moment or two he thought he was back home in Starpoint in the aftermath of the Sardar attack.

Then he realised he was in Ghadra, not the Outlands, and he saw people desperately scrabbling to find the quickest way off the Flats, away from the mad people, the dying and the dead. The dead. Out of the blue it struck Haden that Usshien had been behind the wall where the explosion had happened, and there was no way he could have survived such destruction.

Usshien was dead.

It was over.

Haden Akatine had got his revenge!

The fact that it hadn't come from his own hand only slightly masked Haden's feelings of euphoria and sense of satisfaction that the man responsible for ripping his life apart had himself been torn to pieces. He was standing, transfixed, when a pair of hands grabbed his shoulders from behind, spinning him round. He found himself looking at Decker, his eyes wild, blood trickling from both ears and one nostril.

Decker's face was set in a silent, desperate howl, his fingers jabbing at his mouth, and Haden realised his friend thought he was mute again. With no time for explanations he pointed at where Blade was – *that* was where they must go! Wiping his nose, fleetingly aware that he, too, was bleeding, Haden grabbed Decker's arm and started to run towards where the strange tube-like structure still stood on its four legs.

In the silent chaos a pall of light grey smoke rose straight up from behind the remains of the sandbag barricade, and a steady stream of dirt and unidentifiable lumps of organic material rained out of the sky. The Sardar who'd been dealing with Sgt Blade had forgotten about the execution and had joined their surviving comrades who were cautiously investigating the heart of the explosion where Usshien had last been seen, surrounding which was a ragged flower-petal pattern of bodies created by the blast. No one paid Haden and Decker any attention as they hauled themselves up onto the platform.

'It's all right . . . we'll have these ropes off you any minute now . . .' Mowler looked up from trying to undo the cord biting hard into the spy's left-hand wrist to see two dusty, blood-stained people clambering into view.

'Uncle! Look out!' Mowler had seen the sudden, bizarre spate of weird behaviour in the crowd and concluded that these two were obviously dangerous, mad people.

'What?' Esquabar, having as little success as his nephew undoing the rope attached to the spy's right wrist, glanced irritably over his shoulder. He saw the two figures and assumed they must be the Sardar coming back to finish off the spy. Standing up, wishing he had some kind of weapon, Esquabar registered that these people had no tattoos on the faces.

'Who are you, what d'you want?'

'Can't hear!' Shouting unnecessarily loudly the shorter of the two shook his head and pointed at his ears. 'We've come to rescue our friend!' he pointed at the spy and took a dagger out of his belt. Kneeling down he sliced through the ropes at her ankles, as his taller, red-headed friend removed the gag both Esquabar and Mowler had forgotten to take off.

'Sgt Blade!' yelled Decker. 'Are you all right?'

Before Blade had a chance to answer the platform shuddered, one side dropping an inch, then two more, as jagged cracks split a number of the bigger stone blocks. Above them the rocket lurched sideways. Esquabar ran to the edge of the platform and saw that a fissure about a foot wide had opened up in the Flats and he knew that it had to have been caused by the explosion. It was clear that any minute now a significant part of the plateau was going to break off and plummet into the gorge, taking them with it.

Added to which, the rocket was about to tip over. Which would undoubtedly cause it to explode. As it held at *least* four times as much Phyre as the two barrels that had reduced Usshien to grit, getting as far away as possible, as soon as possible, was of paramount importance.

Esquabar broke out into a cold sweat. He did not want to die – not here in Ghadra anyway – he wanted to get away from this place, with his gold and his diamonds, and live a long and happy life! And there was Mowler – he'd *promised* his sister he'd look after him! The panic gripped him like a vice, his own escape being all he could think of.

'Run!' Esquabar screamed at Mowler as he jumped off the platform. 'Run for your life!'

As he took off after his uncle Mowler shouted a warning but, crouched under the rocket and still deafened, Haden and Decker didn't hear it. Unaware of the imminent danger they were in, it was only once they'd freed Blade and Decker had picked her up that they realised Esquabar and his helper had gone.

'Look!' Haden said, not yelling quite so loudly now that his hearing was beginning to come back.

Some way away now Esquabar and his assistant, their arms and legs a blur as they ran full tilt, were making for nearest gateway. Beneath him Haden felt the increasingly precarious surface of the platform shift again and noticed a couple of Sardar were looking their way and pointing.

'Time we went, Deck!' Haden sheathed his dagger and picked up his pistol. 'Cos I get the feeling those two know something we don't . . .'

The old man stood up and straightened his back very slowly, massaging the base of his spine as he went over to the picture window and its view of his well-tended garden, at the bottom of which, beyond the trees, was a small, fast-running brook. He did love this place.

'I need a walk,' he said, grimacing slightly.

'But you can't stop now, Grampa Savrian!' Mykel shot off the sofa. 'What happened?'

'Come with me and I'll tell you.'

'Did the rocket explode, Grampa?'

The old man nodded. 'People here said say it sounded like distant thunder, apparently.'

'They heard it here?'

'That's right. And I can believe that's true . . . I've been told it was like a couple of volcanoes erupting one after the other – and then, on the horizon, people saw a huge pall of black smoke.'

'So what happened next?' Mykel opened the door for his grandfather and followed him out onto the wide veranda.

'Well, when the rocket blew up, the explosion caused the city to virtually split in half – that fissure I told you about?'

Mykel nodded.

'It was a natural fault in the structure of the rock up there in the Karpak mountains and Ghadra had been built right on it, so when the Phyre in the rocket's fuel tanks ignited there was an explosion so bright it was like another sun, and a great slice of the mountainside – weakened by the first blast, the one that killed Usshien – just came loose and fell away. An awful lot of the city went with it . . . an awful lot.'

'It must've been scary, Grampa . . .'

'Scary? Oh yes . . .' the old man nodded, his lips pursed. 'The ground shook like it was made of porridge, the air split with the most tumultous noise, which was followed by the strangest moment of calm when nothing happened, nothing at all. And then . . . and then it seemed like all Hell broke loose. So many buildings just disappeared, crashing down the mountain, and many of the buildings that were left simply collapsed, killing anyone inside.

'Fires seemed to break out everywhere, parts of what was left of the city becoming a blazing inferno, the smoke and the dust making it almost impossible to see or breathe. A lot of people died that day. By nightfall, when the wind had died down, the place was like a funeral pyre. As a sickle moon came up, all you could hear was people crying and dogs howling. It was terrible.'

'But what happened to Decker and Haden and everyone . . . I mean, did they all get to somewhere safe?'

The old man stopped walking and frowned, chewing on his moustache as he looked off across the valley.

'No,' he said quietly. 'No, they didn't, I'm afraid.'

'Oh . . .' Mykel stared up at his grandfather; was he sad, or did he have something in his eye?

'Unfortunately, the Fates are never kind to everyone,' the old man took a deep breath, patted his grandson on the shoulder and began walking again. 'Pero Esquabar ended up on the wrong side of the fault and was swept away in the avalanche of streets and buildings that got dragged down the mountainside, along with hundreds, maybe thousands of others. And poor Sgt Blade . . .'

'What happened to her?'

'She died a few hours later, from the terrible beating the Sardar had given her.'

'Oh.' Mykel was used to his grandfather's stories being fairly bloodthirsty, but this one was somehow different. 'What about Haden, and Decker – and Mowler, what happened to him?'

'Ah, Mowler . . . the stars really were on that young man's side that day.'

'How'd you mean?'

'He'd been following his uncle, but then got lost in the commotion. Clouds of dust everywhere, people running hither and thither, confusion and panic – no wonder he got disoriented, I suppose, but it was lucky he did.'

'Otherwise he'd have died, with his uncle?'

'Exactly . . . instead, he stayed on the right side of the fault – but only just.'

Mykel frowned. 'Only just?'

'He ran down a street, roof tiles falling around him as buildings caved in, turned to go the way he thought Esquabar had gone and almost careered off the edge of the precipice. Haden and Decker found him, clinging on for dear life, probably minutes from losing his grip and falling to his death. They were the ones who pulled him to safety. It's strange, sometimes, how things work out.'

'Did they find the gold and diamonds, or had Esquabar's building gone?'

'It was still there, although it'd been badly damaged. They

managed to get in and find the gold and diamonds – and later some horses – and get away safely.'

'Did they share?'

'They did. Equally.'

The two of them had reached the trees and walked along a narrow path to a wooden seat, positioned to give a good view of the brook. The old man sat down, while Mykel knelt to look at the water rushing like solid air over the rocks and stones.

'I almost forgot!' Mykel sat back on his heels. 'Tybal! What about Tybal, and Match?'

'Match? I've no idea what happened to her.' The old man smoothed his beard. 'The inn where they'd left her guarding everything was one of the many buildings destroyed that day; it was just a pile of rubble when they got back to it. But come the evening Tybal found them! He must've managed to fly off somewhere safe, but returned later – they heard him around nightfall, a voice in the dusk still telling anyone who'd listen that he was going insane.' The old man smiled at the memory. 'He wasn't going anywhere without Haden – rode all the way back to Quadrine on his shoulder!'

'How long ago did he die?'

'Tybal? He's still alive, last thing I heard.'

'Alive? But . . .' Mykel's face was a picture of confusion.

'Yes?'

'Where is he, then?'

It was the old man's turn to look a bit bewildered. 'You think he should be here?'

'But I thought you were Haden, Grampa!'

'Me?' the old man's face broke into a huge grin and he burst out laughing, slapping his thigh and hee-hawing like a donkey. 'No, son, I'm not Haden!'

'But who . . .'

'I'm Mowler, son . . . that was the nickname my mother had for me . . . never did find out why she used to call me that,' the old man stared off into the middle distance for a second or two then grinned at his grandson, 'Savrian Bellmer, at your service young man! Unlike Haden, who chose to risk everything – first for revenge and then to repay his father's debt – I simply found myself in the middle of all that pandemonium.

'I've never been one to go looking for trouble, although I must say I do remember with some fondness our journey back here to Quadrine. We did have some times! After my experiences in Ghadra, I stuck to science and left the adventuring to Haden and Decker.'

Mykel could not hide his scepticism.

'I promise, hand on heart, that this entire story is true, no matter what you think . . .' The old man took hand off his chest, put it in his pocket and brought out a shiny nugget of yellow metal. 'I made that yesterday – want to see how?'

Why not check out other great books from
Catnip Publishing . . .

STRANGE HIDING PLACE

GRAHAM MARKS

Eleven years ago aliens from another
planet came to Earth to hide something.
They chose a place so strange and
unlikely that their secret would stay
hidden and safe for ever.

Now they need it back. But their
arch-enemies want it too.

As Earth becomes a battleground one boy is
caught up in the very heart of the fighting.
Does Dez have the strength to survive?

The future of more than his own
planet depends on him.

FAULTLINE

GRAHAM MARKS

In California the one thing you
can be sure of is the past. At least
that's what Jamie Delgado's always thought.
Until the day a pack of dinosaurs causes
mayhem in a quiet park.

Someone, somewhere has learned
how to use history as a weapon. And the
result is going to be destruction
on a massive scale.

Unless Jamie can stop them . . .

TAKEDOWN

GRAHAM MARKS

It's 2667 and time is running out for
the human race.

The safety of the world is in the hands
of one man, a soldier more used to
taking life than saving it.

In turn, he has to rely on a sixteen-year-old boy.
The two are going to get closer
than they ever thought possible.

"A dark, paranoid thriller – I loved it!"
PHILIP REEVE

Dragon Racer

MARGARET BATESON-HILL

Joanna Morris's life is about to change for ever. School, homework, even family take second place when she shoots to stardom as the youngest racing-dragon flyer in the country.

Flying Excelsior, the beautiful silver spiked-back dragon, is more exciting that anything she's ever known, and he's soon the best friend she's ever had.

But beneath the glamour and beauty of dragon racing lie terrible jealousies and resentments and Joanna and Excelsior are soon in grave danger.

"An out-of-this-world-exciting story about friendship and loyalty." LOVEREADING4KIDS

J. D. IRWIN

Edwin Spencer has enough problems at
school as it is without strange voices calling
him into another dimension!

But when he is sucked into the peculiar
kingdom of Hysteria on a secret mission he
feels very at home. This could be his chance at
last to be a hero – even if he does have Perpetua
Allbright, school swot as his sidekick.

*"Adventure, time-travel, parallel worlds and laugh-
out-loud humour – what more could you want?"*
Tbk mag

For more information about these
titles and more visit

www.catnippublishing.co.uk